NOEL FITZPATRICK

Illustrated by James Lancett

VETMAN

AND HIS
BIONIC ANIMAL CLAN

HODDER CHILDREN'S BOOKS

First published in Great Britain in 2021 by Hodder & Stoughton Limited

1 3 5 7 9 10 8 6 4 2

Text copyright © Noel Fitzpatrick, 2021
Vetman is a registered trademark of Noel Fitzpatrick
Illustrations © James Lancett, 2021

Special thanks to Michael Ford,
my incredible editor – NF

The moral rights of the author and illustrator have been asserted.

A CIP catalogue record for this book
is available from the British Library.

HB ISBN 978 1 444 96590 2
Trade PB ISBN 978 1 444 96591 9
Signed Edition ISBN 978 1 444 96755 5

Typeset in Adobe Garamond Pro by
Palimpsest Book Production Ltd, Falkirk, Stirlingshire

Printed and bound in Great Britain by Clays Ltd, Elcograf S.p.A.

The paper and board used in this book
are made from wood from responsible sources.

Hodder Children's Books
An imprint of
Hachette Children's Group
Part of Hodder & Stoughton Limited
Carmelite House
50 Victoria Embankment
London EC4Y 0DZ

An Hachette UK Company
www.hachette.co.uk

www.hachettechildrens.co.uk

To every child
that has ever felt not good enough,
who believes in unconditional love with an animal friend,
who believes that animals can save us from ourselves,
and who needs to know that you have a hero inside you
that can conquer any fear.

You are whoever you want to become.
I believe in you. And I am by your side.

Also

To the ten-year-old me in 1978 who wished on the brightest
star in heaven that I might be strong enough and brave
enough – and dreamed up Vetman as my hero.

He would encourage everyone to shine a little light,
so that the world might be a better place
– for all of the animals and for all of us too.

The Man With No Name

He mumbled curses as he stamped through the streets, hauling his bulging shopping bags, his tattered black coat and trousers trailing in the sleet and his scrunched-up hat pulled low on his turnip-shaped head. The metal toes of his heavy leather boots echoed off the cobblestones. On the edge of the town square, red-cheeked children were scooping snowballs, and their laughter chimed with the carols coming from the shop doorways that were rimmed with decorations and scribbled with ice. Mums and dads rushed about, their arms full of presents.

How he hated them. How he hated it all. Their

Christmas cheer, their twinkling lights, their tinsel and their laughter. He saw the dogs sitting up peering through bright windows, and the cats preening their long whiskers. He hated them too. He took everything in with his wizened stare. Truly it was the very worst time of year. *Christmas* . . . Even the word tasted foul in his mouth.

If anyone had managed to catch a glimpse of the man's shadowy face, they'd have noticed that he was different somehow – maybe not quite human. His eyes were as dark as coal in deep buckets, and his ears were scrunched up like nuggets of cauliflower. His bumpy parsnip nose was covered in pimples and his three chins bristled with tufts of spiky hair. His arms were long, with big shovel-like hands that hung right down to his knees, which bulged out of his ripped trousers, as pale as potatoes peeping through a torn sack. A flock of pigeons pecking at the ground turned as one as he approached. Their normal bravery left them and they took flight, circling high overhead.

The man reached his motorbike, which was dusted with snow, and loaded his purchases into the compartments on either side. Fertiliser, cleaning fluid and a dozen other things besides. He took in the scene one final time with utter disdain – joy and cheer everywhere, filling the streets, seeping around the clock tower, the church, the town hall, the shops and the Christmas tree that stood in the middle of the square, bathing all in its warm glow. He imagined the darkness inside him pouring out and swallowing it all.

The man took off his hat and his tangled mane of grey, dank hair fell loose over his shoulders like limp, rotting lettuce. A young boy wielding a snowball stopped suddenly at the sight of the man's scowling face.

'What are you looking at?' snapped the man.

The little boy dropped the snowball and turned away.

The man shoved his scrunched-up hat inside his coat, pulled on his motorcycle helmet and swung his leg over the saddle. With two thrusts of his heel, the bike burst into life, coughing out thick black smoke

into the night sky and spitting dirty cinders into the white snow as it growled away and out of the village.

The pigeons did not land again until he was gone.

The fire inside the man's chest grew like a volcano of hatred as he left town and wound his way through the empty country roads. The bike's headlights picked out the cascading flakes of snow and a strip of tarmac as black as his heart.

Now he had *everything* he needed, every ingredient to take away their happiness and cast their Christmas in shadow. In a week's time, in thousands of homes across the land, their tears would fall just like the snow.

The Man With No Name felt his thick lips curl into a rarely used smile.

It was going to be glorious. His crowning triumph.

Suddenly, as he rounded a bend, a small hunched-up shape was struggling through the snow in a panicked shuffle to cross the road. A hedgehog, disturbed no doubt from his winter hibernation.

The Man With No Name didn't even need to think. With barely a twitch of his lanky arms, he adjusted his front wheel and drove straight at the tiny, terrified creature. The fleeing and flailing limbs of the poor little hedgehog were not quick enough.

He felt a very satisfying bump under the front wheel, and he didn't even bother to look back.

His day was turning out even better than expected.

Chapter 1

Pirate leapt up on his back legs and pawed the mesh door of his pen, like he always did when Imogen came on her rounds. Ciara, the lady who ran Pet Haven, said that he was one of the cleverest and bravest dogs she had ever had the privilege of rescuing, and she'd been doing it for over thirty years! Pirate had had a tough start in life when he was abandoned by the side of a lonely road in the dark, and he was just grateful to have a roof over his head and some cuddles.

All the other dogs were barking and howling now they'd seen the big sack of food that Imogen pushed along on her trolley, but not Pirate. He cocked his black-and-white bristly head to one side in that cute way that only he could and just panted, his tail whipping back and forth. Imogen set down the trolley and stroked his muzzle through the bars of the gate.

'Hello, boy,' she said. 'Sorry I didn't come sooner. I was busy cleaning out the pens. You ready for your walk?'

As Imogen picked up a lead from a peg nearby, Pirate's tail wagged even more furiously.

She'd been coming to Pet Haven for almost six months now, four times a week, since the summer. Volunteering had been her mum's idea, when Imogen had been pestering to have her own doggie friend. Mum thought actually seeing what the responsibility was like might put her off the idea – walking whatever the weather, picking up dog poo, maybe not being able to do things because her dog would need looking after. But Imogen never saw any of her responsibilities as a chore – she saw them as a privilege. In fact, Imogen

loved everything about the rescue and rehoming centre: feeding, cleaning the pens, grooming and clipping nails, helping to build play areas . . . For her, being with the animals was way better than being with any humans anywhere.

And she adored all the dogs, whatever the breed, from the small Chihuahua who yapped all the time, to the lolloping Great Dane with his big tongue that slobbered everywhere. Pirate, though, was her favourite. He was a collie sheepdog with a white face and a black patch of fur over his left eye. He wasn't young but wasn't old either; nobody knew his real age. Even after Imogen brushed his hair – which she regularly did, and he loved it – Pirate was *always* scruffy. As Imogen fixed the lead to his collar, he was bouncing around on his paws.

'You want your coat?' she said. 'It's cold out there.'

But Pirate was already pulling towards the door, heading for the big field.

Walking the dogs was Imogen's favourite part. She could have spent her entire life in the field, watching the dogs running around together as they were sniffing in the hedgerows and enjoying every single moment of freedom. As she and Pirate walked together, she would talk to him, telling him about her day at school, the things that made her happy and the things that made her worried. He would cock his head and prick his ears, and she was sure he understood in his own way.

There were all kinds of dogs at the sanctuary, from puppies that were given up, to dogs left behind when someone had died or couldn't look after them any more. Sometimes it was worse, and the animals that came in had been neglected. That broke Imogen's heart. Some poor dogs and cats had faced difficulties and trauma that left them wary and afraid of humans and other animals, snarling and scratching and even trying to bite. Ciara explained to Imogen that all of them really just wanted badly to feel safe and loved. Deep down, isn't that what everyone wants?

Every week, people wanting to adopt dogs or cats would come to Pet Haven. Sometimes they'd foster a dog for a few days before making a decision. It was normally the cutest or quirkiest or youngest dogs that found a home easily. It was more difficult for older, scruffy ones like Pirate, who'd come in when his elderly mum had died. Ciara's policy was that she'd never put a dog or cat to sleep unless it was very sick and in pain, but money at the sanctuary was always a huge struggle. They relied on donations, and Imogen wanted to do all she could to help. One time she baked cookies for the garden fete – each shaped like Pirate, of course. Another time she made a flower bed out the back in the field and then potted the plants in little containers for a flower sale. Her dad had always been in the garden, and he'd said she had green fingers too.

When it was time to leave at three o'clock, Imogen gave Pirate a last huge cuddle before she closed the gate of his pen.

'Sorry, Pirate,' she said. 'Thank you for talking with me. I'll see you very soon.'

He licked her hand and whined. This was always the worst moment.

'One day you'll come home with me,' Imogen whispered. 'I promise.'

Pirate's tail wagged in understanding.

Imogen gave Ciara a wave as she ran towards the entrance.

'Thanks again, Immy!' Ciara called after her. 'See you soon.'

When Imogen got outside she saw that there was a Christmas tree strapped to the roof rack of their car. Mum had been to the garden centre. Imogen climbed into the front with her mum. Findlay, her brother, was on his game console, as usual, in the back seat.

'Hey,' said Imogen.

Her brother didn't even say hello. His brown fringe practically covered his eyes. Findlay was like that a lot of the time – in his own world. It was worse since Dad had died.

As her mum pulled away, a flash caught Imogen's eye. There was a large black bird, a crow, she thought, standing very still on the roof of the kennels. Only its head moved, twitching from side to side. Then it stared at her. There was a red gleam in its eyes, but it must have been a trick of the light. She felt a shiver.

'You want the good news or the bad news?' said Mum.

'Start with the good,' said Imogen.

'Well, I found the tree decorations in the garage.'

'And the bad?'

'There must have been a mouse in there.'

'Oh, cute!'

Mum frowned. 'Maybe. But it's chewed up half the decorations.'

'Can we get some more?'

'The shops are all sold out,' said her mum. 'I thought you could collect some pine cones from the bottom of the garden and we could paint them?'

'Sure,' Imogen smiled. It sounded pretty boring if she was honest – the sort of thing little kids enjoyed – but she didn't want to upset her mum.

Chapter 1

As they pulled away, she looked back and saw the strange crow had disappeared.

Chapter 2

When they got home, Imogen went into the garden while Mum brought the tree indoors. It wasn't as big as the one they'd had last year, but lots of things were different now Dad wasn't around. Normally they'd all have decorated the tree together, with Dad lifting Findlay to place the star at the top, so it was a good job the tree was smaller, because Mum couldn't lift her brother any more.

Their garden was long and thin, like all the others in their row of houses. In the last few months it had grown quite wild. In many ways, Imogen preferred it like that. She liked things scruffy – maybe that was one of the reasons why she liked Pirate so much. The overgrowth meant even more wild animals. Imogen had discovered many interesting insects in the long grass, and some frogs from the neighbour's pond had sought out the puddle of water beyond the reeds near the bottom fence. One night, looking from her bedroom window, she'd even seen a fox sniffing around the patio.

At the very back of the garden stood an old chestnut tree, and in the fork of its trunk Dad had built a tree house. He'd taught them how to climb up safely too. Imogen had been scared at first, but he'd stood at the bottom, telling her she could do it. 'Every little fear faced fills your heart with courage,' he used to say.

Mum didn't like them climbing up there any more – she said it was too dangerous. The branches of the chestnut reached over the fence into an area that Imogen called the Wilderness. Really it was just a patch of fir trees and thickets about thirty metres across. In the summer it was filled with singing birds, but in winter it was dark and empty of life.

Mum and Dad had always been very strict about the Wilderness – under no circumstances were Imogen and Findlay allowed to climb over the fence. Mum had once told them that a troll lived in the trees, and that he would gobble up any children who came near. But Imogen knew the real reason was that the main road was on the far side, where the cars drove fast and there was no pavement. A few weeks ago, Findlay's football had gone over. Dad normally would have gone to get it back, but for all Imogen knew it was still there among the trees.

Dusk was draining the colour from the sky, revealing the faint outline of the moon. Imogen stooped to gather pine cones to make the decorations but her mind was elsewhere. On Pirate, to be precise. She couldn't bear the thought of him spending Christmas at Pet Haven. And the whole point of volunteering there had been to show her mum how she was ready to look after a dog for real. She knew Mum couldn't have forgotten. As she fumbled through the undergrowth, she firmly made the decision in her head – after dinner, when she was doing the washing up, she was going to ask Mum if she could adopt Pirate and bring him home to live with them. Mum was always in her best mood when Imogen was doing the washing up, like Dad used to do. She *had* to say yes.

Her reverie was interrupted by a sudden buzzing sound. Something whacked into her ankle.

'Ouch!'

She looked down and saw Findlay's chunky-wheeled radio-controlled truck beside her foot. She reached down and picked it up, just as he came running up past the pond with a cheeky grin. The wheels spun in her hand.

'You did that on purpose,' said Imogen. 'I ought to . . .' She looked at the fence and the trees beyond.

'I ought to chuck it in the Wilderness.' She drew back her arm.

'No!' cried Findlay. 'Don't!'

His big brown eyes filled up with tears and Imogen lowered her arm, feeling guilty. Findlay was always crying these days, over the smallest things. Sometimes it could be really annoying.

'Hey, silly! I was only joking.'

She set the truck down again and Findlay sulked. He steered the car away and it bounced over the rough ground. Imogen wanted to put her arm around her brother, but she knew he'd just push her away. Findlay didn't do hugs.

Then she heard another sound. It was a quiet kind of groan at first, but then a bit like a squeal.

'Turn off the car,' said Imogen.

Findlay ignored her, so she grabbed the controller.

'Give it back!' he said, jumping at her.

'Listen!' said Imogen.

Findlay stopped. There was no sound at first, other than the swish of distant traffic on the main road beyond the wood. But then it happened again: a horrible high-pitched moan – and not human. It was coming from the Wilderness.

Findlay swallowed. 'Is it the troll?'

Imogen chuckled, but in truth she was afraid herself. The noise wasn't like anything she'd ever heard before. And it was close. *Very* close. It seemed as if it was just the other side of the weathered fence.

'I'm going to look,' Imogen said.

'You can't!' said Findlay quickly. 'Mum said—'

'I'm not going to go *over* the fence,' said Imogen, walking to the chestnut tree. 'I'm just going to see if I can see anything.'

Findlay looked back towards the house, as if he was thinking about telling on her anyway.

'Don't be such a coward,' she said crossly.

Dad had cut grooves in the trunk of the chestnut

to climb to the tree-house platform, and she scrambled up quickly. She couldn't quite see over the fence from there, so she clambered out along a branch, with her legs straddling either side.

'Be careful,' said her brother.

Imogen edged further, feeling the branch creak a little as it narrowed. She was almost over the fence. Just a little more. On the other side, the fir trees looked like rigid frozen statues, glistening with ice as dusk stole the last remaining warmth of the day. The ground between the trees was thick with thorny undergrowth.

'Can you see anything?' called Findlay.

Imogen frowned and shook her head. She couldn't hear the noise any more either. In the tree above, though, a squirrel bounced between the branches and came to a standstill almost directly overhead. Her tail was very large indeed – almost like one of those brushes Imogen's mum used to clean out deep glasses when they were doing the washing up. She hadn't seen any squirrels in these trees for months.

'Did you hear it too?' Imogen asked the creature.

Unsurprisingly, the squirrel didn't answer.

Chapter 2

Imogen listened for a few seconds more, but there was no sound at all. Now she just needed to shuffle back again. But as she adjusted her body, the branch under her split with a sound like a firecracker. Her heart jumped into her mouth as it gave way.

Imogen screamed as she toppled upside down, tumbling into the Wilderness below.

Chapter 3

She landed in a heap among damp leaves and tangled brambles. For a moment Imogen lay still, catching her breath and hoping nothing was broken. Above her, the squirrel danced away along the branches, her tail sparkling in the faint moonlight.

Then, from the other end of the garden, her mum's panicked voice cried out from the back door.

'Imogen? Findlay? What on earth . . .?'

Imogen picked herself up, untangled the sleeve of her shirt from a large thorny tendril and brushed the leaf mulch off her clothes. The branch she'd been on had knocked over one of the fence panels too. Findlay was staring at her from the other side, his eyes as wide as saucers.

'Are you all right?'

Imogen blushed. 'Fine,' she said, climbing back through into the garden.

Mum was marching down the patio path in her slippers. 'What happened? What was that noise? What are you two up to?'

'We heard a noise,' said her brother.

'A noise that knocked down the fence?' said Mum, finally arriving and folding her arms.

'I wanted to look,' said Imogen. 'I climbed the tree, an—'

'I've told you a hundred times not to—'

Suddenly a keening cry cut her off. They all looked in the direction of the Wilderness.

'Told you,' said Imogen.

'You stay put,' said Mum, and she edged to the gap and stepped over the broken fence panel.

But Imogen didn't stay put. She followed, with Findlay at her side. And it was then that she saw him.

There, nestled at the bottom of one of the tall trees, half covered with leaves, was a tiny hedgehog, just the size of a grapefruit, with a slender black nose testing the air. Imogen crouched beside the little creature. When he saw her, he turned and tried to scurry away, but he couldn't. He let out another wail, and straight away Imogen could see that something was wrong. His back legs weren't working – they just dragged on the ground behind him.

'Poor little fellow!'

She reached out towards the hedgehog and he flexed his spiny back, curling up tightly into a ball.

'Don't touch him,' said Mum. 'They're riddled with fleas.'

'But, Mum, he's hurt,' said Imogen. Her mum was like this with all animals – even tiny spiders. 'He should be hibernating. Something must have woken him up.'

Imogen delicately reached out her fingers and touched the stiff bristles. With her other hand, she rolled the hedgehog slowly into her palm.

'What are you doing?' asked Findlay.

Mum's mouth was flapping as if she wanted to say something but couldn't find the words.

'We need to keep him warm,' said Imogen. 'And we need to find a vet, straight away.'

Calmly, she cradled the little ball of bristles in her

arms, then she stood up and strode back towards the house. Findley grabbed his truck as they all headed back to the light of the back door.

While Mum phoned around for a vet, Imogen and Findlay found a shoebox under the stairs and lined it with an old fluffy towel. Imogen placed the tiny hedgehog gently inside. All the while, she whispered that everything was going to be all right, and that she would look after him.

'I don't think he speaks English,' muttered Findlay.

'The words aren't important,' said Imogen, holding the box on her lap. 'It's the way you say them.'

Mum came in, still holding the phone. 'Sorry, Immy – all the vets are closed. I'm not sure there's much we can do until morning.'

Imogen's heart sank. Then, as she looked at her new little friend, she had a thought. 'I bet Ciara will know what to do!'

Mum didn't look convinced, but nodded. 'It's worth a try, I suppose. Here, use my phone.'

Imogen dialled Ciara's number and explained what had happened. But Ciara sounded glum too. 'If his legs are broken, there's not much a vet can do, I'm afraid. They'll probably have to give the poor mite an injection and put him to sleep. It might be the kindest thing – to end his suffering. We can't leave him in pain, now, can we, sweetie?'

Imogen felt tears in her eyes. 'No, I suppose not.'

'I know it's horrible,' said Ciara. 'Why don't you bring him in tomorrow and I'll ask one of the vets on his rounds to have a look at him.'

'OK,' said Imogen, though she didn't want to think about it. 'He must be hungry, I think. What food can I give him?'

'If you've got some dog or cat food, that won't do any harm,' said Ciara. 'Or maybe a banana or some berries. But just water to drink, not milk.'

Imogen thanked her and looked again at the little hedgehog. While she'd been on the phone, he had unfurled his body and was nuzzling at the edge of the towel with his snout. His tiny black eyes were like perfect polished marbles and they looked at her as if he knew exactly what Imogen was trying to do for him.

She found some dog biscuits in her bag and broke one up into small pieces, placing them in front of the little hedgehog, who sniffed cautiously and ignored them. She filled a shallow saucer with water. The hedgehog drank a little, lapping with his pink tongue.

At dinner, Imogen couldn't eat a thing either. As soon as her mother would let her leave the table, she rushed back upstairs to check on the hedgehog. He seemed to be asleep, but the dog biscuit had been nibbled. While Findlay and Mum decorated the tree together with what was left of the decorations, she stayed by the hedgehog's side. Every so often he would try to get himself more comfortable and instead let out a pained squeal. Imogen sat by the shoebox, watching him and wishing there was more she could do to help. It seemed to her that his noises were getting

weaker all the time. 'Be brave, little one,' she whispered. 'Be strong.'

At bedtime, Findlay came up to the bedroom. In the nights after Dad's death, Imogen's brother had been afraid to sleep alone, so they'd moved a blow-up bed into her room. Now, even though it was months later, it was still there. Imogen didn't mind, really, even though it meant she had less space. She didn't let on that she was afraid too. Findlay went to sleep quickly, with the hedgehog nestled in the box between their beds.

But Imogen couldn't settle. She was worried something might happen to the hedgehog if she drifted off. He wasn't making any noise at all now.

Mum appeared at the door at ten o'clock. 'Time to sleep, sweetheart,' she said.

'Mum, we *can't* have him put down!' said Imogen tearfully.

Her mum sat down on the side of Imogen's bed and looked into the box. 'He's a wild animal, darling,' she whispered. 'If you hadn't found him, nature would have taken its course anyway. That's just how it is.'

'But I *did* find him,' said Imogen. 'That's got to mean something.'

Her mum stroked her hair. 'It means you've got a kind soul, Immy, but you can't work miracles, sweetheart.' She pointed to the open curtains. Outside it was now a cloudless night, the stars like a sprinkling of diamond dust. 'Shall I close them?'

'No, thank you,' said Imogen. 'I like it like that.'

Mum kissed her goodnight and left, and Imogen lay back, looking out at the clear winter sky. One night when she and Dad had been camping the summer before, when he was getting ill but could still move about without much pain, he had told her the names of all the constellations. Her favourite was Canis Major, because it meant 'Big Dog' and was supposed to be shaped like one. Dad had said that the constellation Canis Major contained the Dog Star, also called Sirius, which meant 'sparkling', because it was the brightest star in the night sky.

They'd been lying on the grass outside their tent, because it was still warm after the sunny day.

'You know that's where we all came from, Immy?' her dad had said. 'Up there.'

'Where? The sky?'

'The stars.'

'No, we didn't,' she'd said with a laugh. 'We're not aliens.'

'Everything came from the stars,' said Dad. 'Everything on this planet and every other planet. Every person and every animal. We all come from the same giant explosion thirteen billion years ago. Each and every atom that makes up your body, every chemical in your brain, every feeling you have, it's all just stardust, really. Just stardust, forged in the fires of heaven.'

'Even love?'

'Oh, especially love. Up there, we are all one. We came from one and we go back to one. I will always be there, looking down on you.'

They'd lain there for a moment, staring out, until Imogen had spoken the words that had been lurking. She'd been trying to keep them in, to be a big girl who didn't cry and didn't say silly things.

'I don't want you to die, Daddy. I'm scared.'

He'd pulled her closer to him. 'I know you are. But I want you to remember something. Bodies don't always work properly. Sometimes they go wrong, and it's annoying and sad and unfair, and people die. But love doesn't die. Love never dies. Love is too pure for that. Love is eternal.'

'You promise?'

'I swear it on the Dog Star,' he'd said. 'Love is in the stars, Immy. It really is. Just look up and you'll see it.'

Even though she knew he was only trying to make her feel better, she'd nodded. The least she could do was try to make him feel a little better too.

* * *

'Wake up!'

Imogen woke with a start and found Findlay standing over her. His cold hand was on her arm and the bedside lamp was on, making her squint. She looked at her clock and saw it was just after midnight. Her first thought was the hedgehog. Something bad must have happened. Or maybe Findlay had wet the bed again.

But Findlay was just standing there stammering, trying to get something out but not quite able to say it. He was pointing at the window.

'Sq . . . squ . . . there's a squ . . .'

There, standing on the outside sill, was a squirrel.

And not just any squirrel. It was the squirrel from earlier in the Wilderness. She was using her weird tail to hit the window, twirling back and forth like the bristles of a drive-through carwash.

'Am I dreaming?' said Imogen. 'Pinch me.'

Findlay pinched her arm.

'Ouch! It's just a figure of speech, Finn.'

'What does she want?' asked her brother.

'How should I know?' Imogen swung her legs out

of bed and the squirrel moved her head to follow her. 'I'm going to open the window.'

'Don't!' said her brother.

'It's only a squirrel!'

She expected the squirrel to bolt away as she reached for the window handle but she didn't budge at all. Clearly she was very tame – maybe one of the squirrels from the local park, used to being fed. Imogen opened the window and the squirrel hopped in, followed by a blast of cold air. Findlay let out a shriek as the squirrel bounced over the bedside table, on to the bed, then along a bookshelf and finally on to the floor, making a scratching, swirling sound with her tail, twittering as if she wanted to say something. Then she leapt high, landing beside the shoebox on the carpet. The squirrel reached over the edge of the box with her little paws and sniffed intently, before looking up at Imogen with her tail swishing.

'Do you think . . . they know each other?' asked Findlay.

'Don't be silly,' said Imogen.

Now the squirrel was closer she could see her tail in even more detail. An icy glaze coated the bristles and reflected the light like oil on water, gleaming all the colours of the rainbow. It wasn't covered in fur, but plastic spines on actual wire of some sort. Imogen extended her hand slowly and tentatively brushed it with her fingers. It made no sense at all. 'Steel wire!' she gasped. 'Who'd do such a horrible thing?'

Findlay shrugged.

Then the squirrel did the strangest thing. With her tiny paws clasped over the edge of the box, she braced her back legs against the side of the bed and began to *pull*. The box moved a short distance – a few centimetres – and then again, a little further across the carpet towards the door. Imogen and Findlay were so stunned that they just stood there, mouths open.

'Hey, no!' said Imogen, grabbing the other side of the box.

The squirrel cocked her head belligerently and pulled harder.

'You can't take him,' said Imogen. 'He is very, very sick.'

The squirrel chittered loudly and sounded almost cross. Her tail began to whirr around like a propeller and she pulled harder against Imogen's hand.

'Our hedgehog friend needs to see a vet,' said Imogen sternly.

The squirrel bounded towards the door, climbing up it with a rapid patter of feet and her propeller tail, and then somersaulted backwards.

'Cool!' said Findlay.

The squirrel then rushed back, popped her little paws on the box and pulled again against Imogen's hand, with a very fierce look in her eyes.

'I think she actually wants us to follow,' said Imogen.

She grabbed her jumper and picked up the box with the hedgehog in.

'*Where?*' said Findlay.

Imogen smiled at her brother and shrugged. 'There's only one way to find out.'

Chapter 4

The house was silent; their mum's bedroom door closed. The squirrel seemed to know where she was going as she scuttled along the bannister downstairs, using her propeller tail like a rudder, finally alighting on the front doormat. Cradling the hedgehog carefully in his box, Imogen crept after the squirrel on tiptoes. Findlay paused at the top of the stairs, struggling to get his trainers on.

'Get a move on!' hissed Imogen.

He did as she said, but when he reached her side he whispered, 'We should tell Mum.'

Imogen shook her head. She was worried that the squirrel might run away if she got scared – and that somehow this magical spell, whatever it was, would be broken, never to be found again. 'We're not going far,' she said.

She didn't know that, of course. She didn't know where they were heading at all. Following a magical squirrel into the frosty night was clearly mad, but as she opened the front door and the squirrel scuttled through, Imogen knew she simply had to find out where she had come from. Mum would be furious if she knew they were sneaking out, but the thought of losing their new-found hedgehog friend was even worse.

Imogen grabbed her green woolly coat from the peg in the hallway, and Findlay found his fleece jacket with the floppy hood. The squirrel had already sped off down the street, so Imogen quickly pulled on her wellies. When she got out on to the pavement she could see that the squirrel was waiting for them under the orange glow of a street lamp, her tail twitching furiously, as if beckoning them forward.

The crisp air actually tasted of ice as they both pulled up their hoods and stumbled down the footpath glittering with frost.

'Let's get our bikes,' said Imogen, zipping up her coat and pulling on her gloves.

Findlay didn't argue this time, and they slipped through the side gate to where the bicycles were kept under a lean-to. Imogen's bike was too small for her now, a little babyish. Dad had promised her a new one, so they could go out together on longer rides, but of course that hadn't happened. Fortunately, it had a basket at the front, which was the perfect size for the hedgehog in his box. Off she rode, standing up on the pedals because her legs were too long for her to sit on the saddle. Findlay followed behind.

The squirrel waited for them to catch up, then set off once more.

Many of the houses on the estate had Christmas

lights draped outside, and trees sparkling in their windows, but there was no one about on such a cold night in the early hours. Imogen wondered, though, if someone were to look out, what they'd make of the strange sight of two children on their bicycles pursuing a hopping squirrel down the street.

Their animal guide led them out of the estate and over the deserted roundabout, through the familiar streets of the village. Only they weren't so familiar now, without cars and people. They seemed like another world entirely – a kind of dreamworld. The squirrel didn't appear to tire one bit. If anything, it was they who struggled to keep up as she leapt from wall to bin to railing. And every so often she really did seem to fly, or at least to glide, with the turbo-boost of her propeller tail.

They passed the church, the town hall and the village green, then the squirrel jinked around a corner and on to an unlit country lane. There was no pavement here, and while Imogen felt fearful, she tried not to show it for her brother's sake. They were heading into the unknown, further than Findlay had ever ridden before. Imogen thought of their mum tucked up in bed. She prayed that nothing woke her up.

They travelled further out of town – one mile, maybe more – passing hedgerows, big trees, farmyard gates, and the smokeless chimneys of quiet country houses like shadows lurking ominously beside the road. Gradually the dread in Imogen's gut built until it felt like a solid thing inside her, squirming and uncomfortable. Her fingers, even in her gloves, had grown almost numb with cold, and at last she could bear it no more. She looked back at Findlay, his breath coming in rapid white puffs. His face, under his hood, looked as white as the moon, and his lips had a blue tinge. No, this was too much. Too risky. She desperately wanted the best for her little hedgehog friend, but enough was enough.

She jammed on her brakes, as did Findlay, just as the squirrel darted sideways ahead, disappearing into a hedge. Imogen and her brother rolled up to the same spot and saw there was a narrow gap leading through to a field on the other side. The squirrel was waiting for them on top of a fence

post, perched on her hind legs with her tail buzzing.

Imogen and Findlay pushed their bikes through.

'Where are you taking us?' Imogen asked. The squirrel simply chittered and spun away, heading for some trees on the other side of the field.

They set off again. The ground was uneven and muddy in places, rattling Imogen's bones as she tried to keep up with the squirrel, and her tyres bounced and struggled to grip. As they reached the edge of the woodland, Findlay gave a cry of alarm. Imogen turned to see his front wheel twisted sideways

in a hidden rut. He toppled from the saddle, landing with a dull splat on the muddy ground. She got off her own bike and helped him up. Luckily, he didn't seem hurt at all.

'I want to go home,' he said miserably.

Imogen peered into the shadowy trees. She couldn't see the squirrel at all now, and she felt a spike of panic. 'We've lost her!' she said.

'No – *you've* lost her,' cried Findlay.

'Then go home!' snapped Imogen. 'You're only slowing me down.'

As soon as she said it, she felt bad. He was only eight, after all. His lip began to quiver.

'I don't . . . I don't know the way,' he said.

'I'm sorry,' said Imogen. 'I'm just annoyed we came this far and now it's for nothing.'

'There she is!' said Findlay, pointing past his sister.

Sure enough, the squirrel was back, gripping the

base of a nearby tree trunk and flailing her tail. Imogen grinned, then took a deep breath. 'I know you want to go home. So do I. I really do. But we've come this far. Ten more minutes, OK? Then we turn back.'

Findlay hitched his chin, but looked uncertain. 'Five,' he said.

'Deal,' said Imogen. 'But I think we have to leave the bikes here.'

Imogen gathered up the hedgehog in the towel from inside the shoebox and wrapped him up tightly. Together, side by side, they entered the darkness of the forest.

The squirrel stayed much closer to them now, as if she could sense their fear. As she darted along the forest floor, her tail kicked up clouds of icy frost. Imogen's feet crunched over the ground as they threaded a path in pursuit, ducking between the trees and picking their way around bushes and through snatching brambles. The wood was consumed by a murky fog, with moonlight trickling from the branches above. The smell of musty vegetation filled the air, rising through the frost on the forest floor. Imogen couldn't help but think of all the fairy tales she'd read as a little girl about bad things that happened in forests. And though she felt it was unlikely that there were horrible witches or wolves in this one, her skin still prickled. If there was something in here, whatever it might be, it could be close and they'd never know it.

In time, though, her nose picked up a different smell through the trees. It was like a mixture of woodsmoke and burnt petrol. Very soon the trees thinned out and they entered a clearing where the stars twinkled above in a circle of night sky. There was a small, single-storey stone cottage standing in the centre, surrounded by a thin layer of snow. Grey smoke peeled off from a chimney that sprouted from a roof of thick, uneven slates. The small windows were all dark. At the front, wooden steps led up to a rickety veranda. Imogen had no idea how deep they'd come into the forest, but she noticed there was no road or track approaching the tumbledown house. Whoever lived here probably didn't get many visitors.

She and Findlay both hesitated on the edge of the clearing. The idea of approaching the cottage was beyond daunting. They simply had no clue who – or what – might be inside. But the squirrel had no such qualms and she shot across the ground, scuffing up snow with her tail, and in through a cat flap in the front door. Imogen suddenly had a sinister thought.

What if we've been lured here?

'You stay here,' she said to her brother.

He shook his head briskly. 'No way!'

'OK,' said Imogen, 'but let me do the talking.'

Trying to appear brave, she marched towards the front door, eyes peeled in case of any sudden movement. Soon she was climbing the creaking wooden steps.

Her knees weren't exactly knocking, but her legs felt like jelly as she cradled the hedgehog with one hand and lifted the other to knock. She could hear Findlay's breathing close behind her.

Before her knuckles could fall, a heavy thumping came from the other side of the door, as if some monstrous ogre was rushing to meet them. Imogen took a step back, just as the door was yanked open

from the inside. She stumbled back into Findlay and tripped, and they both ended up on the ground with the poor hedgehog sprawled out on his towel. When she looked up, she let out a terrified gasp.

A man stood inside, haloed in the dim light – or at least he looked like a man. He was wearing a long grey smock that trailed from his neck to his ankles. It was unbuttoned on his upper chest, and beneath it, on some kind of under-shirt, Imogen made out two letters: a 'V' and an 'M'. He had a big mop of tousled grey and black hair on his head. His eyes were wide and crazed – bright green like fierce emeralds, and so intense that Imogen almost felt them burn right through her as he glared at them lying on the ground. He filled the doorway, casting a long shadow from the flickering light behind. He gave the impression of great strength, as though he could rip up a tree stump with his bare hands.

Imogen and Findlay scrambled to their feet, clutching

one another, Imogen carefully scooping the hedgehog up again in the towel.

The man stepped out of the cottage towards the children. His feet were bare on the timbered step. He peered first left and then right, with his brilliant-green eyes narrowing as he took in the scene. His gaze eventually rested on the towel in Imogen's hands, and then softened. 'What is it you have there?'

The voice did not match his appearance at all. It was deep, but soft too, and it seemed to fill the entire clearing.

'It . . . it's a hedgehog,' said Imogen. 'He's hurt.'

The man nodded, and frowned as though he was feeling the pain himself. 'I see . . . I see.'

A long pause settled as Imogen wondered what to do next.

'Well, you have come to the right place,' said the man at last, and a rather gentle smile spread across his unshaven, bristled face. He looked a lot less scary now as he held out both hands – big, strong hands – palms upwards. 'May I have a look?'

Part of Imogen didn't want to give the hedgehog up. She didn't know this man, or anything about him. But, despite her worries, she found herself extending her own hands and placing the little spiky bundle in his. He folded it to his chest as if what was inside was the most delicate and precious creature in the universe. 'There, there,' he mumbled. 'Quite safe now.' With a single finger he pulled the towel aside and smiled. Imogen was astonished to see the hedgehog uncurl his defences at once and touch his moist nose against the man's fingertip.

'Are you a vet?' blurted out Findlay.

The man looked up slowly, as if woken from a daydream. 'Kind of – yes, young man. The animals call me Vetman.'

Findlay's lip curled in confusion. 'How can the

animals call you anything?'

'Well, my real name is hard to pronounce,' said the man.

'That's not what I meant,' said Findlay. 'Animals can't talk!'

The man looked aghast. 'Oh, my young friend, how wrong you are. Animals speak all the time! It's just that sometimes we don't listen – or know how to.' He looked down and smiled sweetly. 'See, this little hedgehog is speaking to us now.'

The hedgehog made small squeaking noises as the man stroked his now-unfurled belly with his finger.

'We followed a squirrel here,' said Imogen. 'Is she yours?'

The man's eyes widened. 'Mine? A squirrel? I'm not sure how that would work.'

'But she's in your house now,' said Imogen.

'And I am in this forest,' said the man. 'Do I *belong* to the trees?'

'Well, no, but . . .'

'We don't own animals, young lady,' said the man. 'Rather, we have the privilege of having their companionship in our lives and on our planet. They look after us when we look after them.'

The Vetman, or whoever he was, looked as if he was about to say something else, when suddenly Findlay's hand gripped Imogen's arm, hard. He was pointing a trembling finger into the cottage. Imogen's eyes fell on something behind the man. Something deeper inside the cottage. Something large, moving in the shifting shadows. *Slithering* . . .

Her brain knew what her eyes were seeing, but at the same time she couldn't quite believe it.

'Is something wrong?' said the man. He turned too. 'Oh yes. Oh dear.'

The alligator – for that's what it undoubtedly was, and which was more than two metres long – began to pad towards them. His thick, scaly tail swayed from side to side, shining like metal, and his claws rattled on the ground.

Imogen couldn't even find a scream, but her legs finally caught up with her terrified thoughts, shuffling backwards. Then, along with her brother, she turned and ran for her life.

Chapter 5

'Come back!' called the man, and his voice seemed to shake the freezing air. Imogen looked over her shoulder and saw that he was running after them with a stumbling, uneven gait. The alligator was coming too and he moved faster than she would have thought possible, his body gleaming in the moonlight. She could see his strange tail flailing through the snow – a metal tail, with long jagged spikes jutting along its length.

Taking Findlay's cold hand, she plunged into the trees. They ran together, feet snagging on roots, twigs whipping at their faces. She had no idea where they were going – back towards the road, or maybe deeper into the forest from which they might never escape. She wanted her mum, but she knew full well her mum was nowhere near.

'Help!' she cried, but her voice seemed swallowed by the night. Still, she called out again. There might be other houses. *Someone* might hear. They ran for what might have been one minute or might have been ten, until each breath was painful in her chest, and then she felt Findlay slowing. 'My shoe!' he said.

'Come on!' she urged him, but she could see he'd lost one of his trainers. She slowed, and he staggered into her.

'I can't!' he said. 'Please, stop.'

They stood for a moment, pressed up against a tree, panting clouds into the stillness. Imogen strained her eyes and ears, but couldn't see or hear anyone following them.

Her heart began to slow. They'd surely lost him. More

Chapter 5

to the point, there was no sign of the giant scaly reptile. Imogen still couldn't believe it. Surely it was illegal to keep such a dangerous animal outside of a zoo!

'Are you OK?' she whispered to Findlay.

He nodded, looking down at his wet and muddy sock. 'We're going home now, aren't we?'

'Absolutely!' she said. All they had to do now was keep going until they found a road, then flag down a passing car. Mum would be really cross, but once they'd called the police and told them about the strange man and his illegal pet, none of that would matter. As for the poor hedgehog . . .

Crack . . .

Both their heads snapped to face one another.

Imogen wasn't sure where the sound had come from, but her ears picked up more. Footsteps, coming through the trees. Findlay gave out a small wail, but she clamped a hand over his mouth. They crouched behind the trunk of a tree.

Peering around it, Imogen saw the man stumble into view. He leaned against a tree with one hand, holding his chest with the other, catching his breath. 'Please,' he said. 'I mean you no harm.'

There was no sign of the alligator, thank goodness. Imogen picked up a fallen branch.

She'd defend herself if she had to. 'I've got a phone,' she shouted. 'I'm calling the police!'

The man turned towards her voice. 'You mustn't,' he cried. 'You can't! It would ruin everything. My life's work! All I've ever—'

His voice became strangled. Imogen looked again and saw the man had fallen to the ground on his knees, where he wheezed. Findlay stared too. 'Is he all right?' he muttered.

Imogen didn't know. He might be trying to trick them, to get them to come close. Her head told her to use the opportunity to escape. To take the safe option.

But her heart told her the opposite. The man pitched forward, rolling on to his back. His breathing was raspy and irregular. He needed an ambulance, but she didn't really have a phone at all to call one.

'What can we do?' she called out.

The man didn't answer. If he was dying, she couldn't simply stand by.

Imogen stepped out from their hiding place, still gripping the branch.

'What are you going to do?' asked Findlay.

She edged towards the prone man, ready to strike or run or both. But the closer she got, the more certain she was that he was not pretending. His eyes were wide – scared, even. They flicked towards her.

'I'll . . . be . . . fine . . .' he said, between shallow breaths. 'Help . . . me . . . sit . . .'

Imogen tossed the stick aside and bent over him. She offered her hand, and he took it in his big palm. Bracing her feet, she pulled him up into a sitting position – which was no mean feat – and then she steadied his back with her other arm. Beads of sweat glistened on his forehead.

'Is it your heart?' she asked, thinking about the way he'd gripped his chest.

'Something like that,' he said.

'Has it happened before?'

'Many times.' He looked at her. 'More these days, unfortunately. Perhaps you'd be kind enough to help me back home?'

Imogen flinched. 'There was an alligator.'

'Indeed, and he will be very pleased to meet you properly.'

'That isn't what I meant. Won't he . . . Won't he eat us?'

The man frowned, as though the thought genuinely hadn't occurred to him. 'I think that's very unlikely.'

Findlay had approached too, and stared in wonder at the man. He was shivering.

'You are cold,' said the strange man. 'Come, we must get you warm.'

Imogen knew he was right. If they stayed outside much longer, her brother might get hypothermia.

'You can trust me,' the man said. 'You really can. I swear.'

Imogen thought to herself that's exactly what a

kidnapper would say, but something in his face made her believe it. His green eyes glowed with what she thought was deep kindness, the likes of which she had never seen before. His mop of pepper-coloured hair and his bristly chin didn't frighten her so much now either. With Findlay's help, she hoisted the man to his feet. He gave a shuddering breath, then nodded through the trees. 'This way.'

His long nightgown snagged in the brambles but it didn't take long at all before they were in the clearing again, finding Findlay's trainer on the way. As they walked towards the house, Imogen's eyes were alive for the alligator, but he was nowhere to be seen. The veranda seemed somewhat more welcoming now and the front door of the cottage was open. Inside, in the hallway, lying on the back of an upside-down wheelbarrow, was the hedgehog in his towel bundle. The squirrel was sitting on her haunches right beside the little creature, as if guarding him. Both were picked out in a spotlight that flashed across the room and into their eyes as they entered. Imogen squinted and threw up a hand against the glare.

'Not so bright, please,' said the man.

The light's intensity dropped and Imogen could see again. Only now she saw that the light was coming from a huge feathered bird perched on a rafter under the roof: a giant tawny owl, to be precise, with tufty feathered ears and left eye aglow, lit by some sort of bulb within.

'Huh?' she said, because it made no sense at all.

'So how is our little visitor?' said the man.

The wheelbarrow on the ground shifted, and Findlay said, 'It's got legs!'

Small legs slowly emerged from underneath the upturned wheelbarrow. Even more amazingly, a small green scaly head with big brown eyes also emerged, with two bumps on the forehead and a beak-like mouth.

The old tortoise smiled up at everyone and began

to waddle across the floor. The wheelbarrow moved too, as if it was fixed over the tortoise's shell. Then the children realised that wasn't it at all . . .

'The wheelbarrow *is* his shell!' Imogen exclaimed.

'*Her* shell, actually,' said the man. 'It was a nasty infection that would have killed her otherwise.'

'So you really are a vet then?' asked Findlay.

The man smiled. 'You can call me Vetman too, if you like, but I'm not really a normal vet.'

'You're telling *me*!' said Imogen.

'A normal vet would have put Ms Tortoise to sleep, and I understand. They have a particular opinion and code they have to follow. But technology moves on, and so I felt that the right thing was to give her quality of life, rather than taking her life away.'

'By attaching a wheelbarrow?'

'That was her choice. There were other options. A lawnmower grass box; a cement mixer bowl.' He looked at the tortoise. 'What was the other one?'

The tortoise made a small clicking sound.

'Oh, that's right! A tombola drum!'

Imogen laughed, but Vetman looked deadly serious.

'So you fixed the squirrel's tail too?' said Findlay.

'And the owl's eye!' said Imogen.

Vetman nodded. 'He came to me half blind after an unfortunate collision with a branch.'

The hedgehog stirred a little in his towel on the back of the tortoise's wheelbarrow.

'So can you help him?' asked Imogen.

'I hope so,' said Vetman. 'We'll need to have a look, won't we?'

He extended his hand, pointing towards an inner door in a dimly lit recess at the back of the hallway.

'Us too?' said Findlay.

'I need all the hands I can get,' said Vetman. 'Not to mention wings and claws.'

Findlay licked his lips nervously. 'We're not vets.'

The strange man grinned. 'You have good hearts,

and that's the most important thing. Not all humans do.'

We really should be getting home, thought Imogen, but she longed to know what was behind the door. A few more minutes couldn't hurt.

'OK,' she said.

Vetman clapped his hands in delight and strode towards the door. He seemed to have recovered from whatever had happened in the woods.

'Are you ready?' he said, gripping a large brown handle on the door. In truth, it looked more like a lever than a handle. The owl flew over and landed on his shoulder, and the squirrel bounced up and down on the back of the wheelbarrow, as Vetman held the little hedgehog in his arms.

'Yes,' said Imogen and Findlay together.

'Very good.'

Vetman pulled the lever, but it wasn't the door that moved.

Chapter 5

Findlay yelped as, with a dull thump, the floor itself juddered and started to move downwards, throwing up dust at the edges. They were standing on a square platform, three or four metres across, descending slowly into a deep shaft beneath the cottage like a sort of elevator platform. Vetman hopped on beside them. The platform gave way into the ground beneath and it seemed as if the cottage around them quite suddenly disappeared as chains rattled noisily over pulleys around the sides of the dark shaft. For a moment, in the blackness, Imogen felt dizzy and lost, too shocked to be afraid. Findlay's eyes sought out hers and she offered a little nod to reassure him.

The platform chugged downwards like a train on rickety tracks for what seemed like a long time but couldn't have been more than a minute or so, and then, slowly, they emerged into a brightly lit space. Imogen gasped, hardly able to take it in.

It was a huge underground cave, with towering walls

of rock on all sides. Here and there were alcoves, and side caverns, and passages large and small, hewn out of the rock and leading off to other chambers. It teemed with animals: birds, mammals and reptiles of all kinds. Many had modifications, just like the owl and the squirrel – metal and plastic and wooden limbs, or various fabrics, materials and what looked like machines grafted on to their bodies. Lush plants sprouted here and there, among equipment that looked like something from a science fiction movie, all polished stainless steel. There were old-fashioned gadgets belching steam as well as more high-tech control panels and computer screens. The alligator that the children had seen earlier relaxed in a swamp at one end, with just the very top of his head and the metal spines on his tail breaking the surface. The air was filled with chirrups and howls, squawks and hisses, as if every creature was welcoming Vetman and his visitors. It was like a zoo, but there were no cages, no

tanks, no fences or nets. All the creatures were free. Findlay's mouth was hanging open but turned slowly into a smile of utter wonderment.

'What is this place?' said Imogen as the elevator platform bumped to a stop.

Vetman leapt off the platform, more agile than she'd seen him before, as though the very air of this place was filling him with new life. He swung his arms open wide as the animals and birds swept towards him in a giant embrace of fur and feathers and scales. Last of all, a small elephant lumbered out from one of the alcoves, flexing an articulated trunk that looked like shining aluminium, and giving a loud trumpet.

'Welcome, my friends,' said Vetman over the din. 'Welcome to the Bionic Bunker!'

Chapter 6

Imogen stared around in astonishment at the variety of creatures. Thoughts of fear, or home, disappeared. The elephant wandered over to the carcass of an old car and began lifting out parts from under the open bonnet with his aluminium trunk, handing them to a monkey who was jumping around on some kind of jointed metal legs.

'Where do all the animals come from?' Imogen asked in a whisper.

'Everywhere,' said Vetman. 'We rescue all the waifs and strays, the animals with no homes and no hope, the rejects and the misfits, the maimed and damaged, the poor creatures with nobody to love them.' A platypus sat on his shoulder and ruffled his unruly hair with her beak. She had what looked like a shiny metal cheese grater on her belly. 'We take them all in. We fix them – legs and tails, trunks and shells. Whatever we can do to make them whole again. In some cases, to make them even better than before.'

'What do you mean, "we"?' asked Imogen. 'Have you got an assistant?'

Before he could answer, there was a sudden whooshing noise and down flew a huge pigeon with metal wings stretched out majestically like a silver fighter jet. Each feather looked like a gleaming arrow, all tightly packed into mechanical folding and flapping wings that glistened as she swooped overhead.

Vetman grinned and spread his arms as wide as the wings of the pigeon. 'Those are titanium wings and these *are* my assistants. Here we all help each other. Cooperation, compassion and understanding – that's the name of our game. I treat them with respect and fairness, I teach them one thing at a time and they all move forward in earnest. Everyone here is equal. There's no judgement of anyone no matter where you might have come from, what colour or species or shape you may be – we all cooperate and help each other out.'

Vetman hummed a happy tune as he skipped through the bionic bunker. 'It's all right, my friends, we're all in it together. We take care of each other – and I'm here to make you better. Human or animal, we're very much alike – whether you've got skin, or feathers, or scales, or wool, or spikes . . . or a big hairy mane . . . we're all equal here and we consider all the same. It's one same medicine for all of us, one same love and one same trust. We're all in it together, humans and animals. We're all in it together, the very best of pals.'

Findlay jerked back as a small rabbit shot past on a turbo-powered hoverboard made from an old hairdryer.

She was followed by a kangaroo bouncing on what looked like a large spacehopper ball.

'How can they help?' he said. 'They're just animals!'

'Just?' said Vetman. He looked at Findlay with a mocking frown. '*Just?* My boy, you humans have forgotten so much.'

Imogen didn't know why he kept talking about them as 'humans' when he was one too.

Vetman clapped his hands together and all of the animals pricked their ears and turned their eyes towards him.

'We have a new patient,' he called. 'Let's prepare!'

And so off he went, scurrying around and pushing

a trolley. The animals seemed to know what to do without being told, and fluttered and scrambled in response, gathering equipment. The kangaroo fetched bottles and jars from a shelf and popped them in her pouch. The rabbit whizzed about, ears flopping in the breeze, gathering needles, forceps and other surgical tools. The pigeon brought drapes and bandages in her beak. The elephant plucked up a tray of metal plates and screws with a grabbing device on the end of his trunk. Imogen giggled a little, because it reminded her of one of the games she never won, where

you had to grab a fluffy toy with a mechanical hand. Then the monkey with the bionic legs pushed an operating table into the centre of the chamber.

Vetman looked at Imogen who was clearly in awe. 'Oh yes,' he said matter-of-factly. 'We have fashioned new legs for him using 3-D printed cobalt-chromium and molybdenum alloy joints. They work quite well, don't they?'

Imogen nodded in amazement – the monkey's legs were as agile as pogo sticks.

Vetman lifted the hedgehog from the tortoise's wheelbarrow and placed him down gently.

'First, we'll need to see what's the matter now, won't we,' said Vetman.

Out of nowhere a large brown-furred bat landed on the end of the operating table and gingerly edged towards the hedgehog. He had a giant mechanical eye that made a whirring sound, then he lifted one of his wings and spread it out wide. The thin membrane of his wing suddenly became luminescent and flickered like a computer screen. Within seconds an X-ray picture appeared on the wing.

'That's amazing!' said Imogen.

Vetman grunted, as though it really wasn't such a big deal that a bat had an X-ray machine for an eye and his wing was the display monitor. Then he studied the image, squinting. 'Oh dear. Yes, I see.'

'Can you make him better?' breathed Findlay.

Vetman smiled and winked kindly at him. 'Sadly not, that's the best image he can produce with that old X-ray machine – I really ought to upgrade it.'

Findlay shook his head. 'No, I meant—'

'It was just a joke,' said Vetman. 'You mean, can I fix his legs? Well, we can certainly try.'

He went to a sink in the wall. 'Since life began on Planet Earth, man was supposed to look after the animals, to lead by example,' said Vetman. 'Sometime, somehow, they forgot. It would be great if people were a little more kind and compassionate and if they treated animal life as less disposable. It's easy to say, sometimes, that *nothing can be done*, when the exact opposite is often true. There's nearly always *something* that can be done. Like I said before, at the end of the day it's all about whether what we're doing is the *right* thing to do. I think our hedgehog friend deserves a chance, don't you?' He held out his hands and the monkey squirted bright-blue liquid on to them. 'Come on, you two,' he said. 'Scrub up.'

Imogen and Findlay looked at each other with a mixture of fear and excitement, not knowing what to expect or what would be expected of them, but ready to help in any way.

'Don't worry,' said Vetman. 'I am by your side; just follow my lead!'

Imogen and Findlay took off their coats and sweaters, joining Vetman at the sink. The monkey squirted their hands too, and they washed them side by side. Imogen watched Vetman closely, copying every move.

'We're not vets, you know?' she said.

'Oh, but you're far more than that,' said Vetman.

The children didn't know what he meant, but carried on as instructed anyway. They all put on surgical masks, then from across the bunker came the flutter of wings. A flock of budgerigars were carrying surgical gowns, and Vetman lifted his arms as they draped a blue gown over him, covering up the V and M on his undershirt, which Imogen could now clearly see was a surgical scrub-top. Vetman put on sterile gloves, also carried by the budgies. Imogen and Findlay did the same, following his instructions to the letter. As Vetman led them back to the operating table, there was a small team of guinea pigs standing by with a pot of brown liquid.

The elephant sauntered over and held up a machine with gas-filled chambers and tubes with his trunk. Imogen flinched as a big furry tarantula crept across the table. Four of her legs were made of delicately jointed metal.

'That's incredible!' said Imogen.

'It's an alloy of vanadium!' said Vetman. 'The strongest man-made metal on Earth.'

The spider used her legs to gingerly fit a mask to the hedgehog's face. The alligator had returned, and in his teeth held a spool of thread. Imogen tried not to look at him as he waited under the table at her feet, his spiked titanium tail lashing slowly from side to side.

Vetman unzipped a case of gleaming tools – scalpels and forceps and tongs as well as other unrecognisable contraptions.

'You don't need to be afraid,' he said. 'I am by your side all the way.'

'I'm not,' Imogen said. But she was lying. What if they got something wrong? What if they did more harm than good?

'Light, please,' said Vetman.

Chapter 6

The owl positioned himself at the head of the table and turned his bright eye on the little hedgehog, who looked so small, desperate and sad.

'Anaesthetic,' said Vetman.

The elephant squeezed the cylinder on the machine in his trunk, and the tube leading to the mask over the hedgehog's face filled with anaesthetic vapour.

'Go to sleep for a while, little one,' said Vetman.

In just a few heartbeats, the hedgehog's eyes drifted closed.

A parrot, with a bright fluorescent crest of red feathers, a huge mechanical beak of silver chrome and claws of steel, flew down from her perch and sliced up surgical drapes, dipping each in a dish of disinfectant before hanging them on a peg. Then the small army of guinea pigs gently scrubbed the tiny broken legs of the hedgehog with the brown solution, which Imogen guessed was iodine, using small swabs of cotton wool. The squirrel, without even needing to be asked, jumped up on Vetman's shoulder and placed a pair of strange glasses over his eyes.

Vetman turned the hedgehog on to his side carefully.

'This poor little fellow has multiple fractures in both legs,' he said. 'Scalpel, please, Imogen.'

Imogen steadied her hands and passed the gleaming instrument.

'Can they be mended?' whispered Findlay.

'Let's see,' said Vetman. He made a delicate incision. 'Vascular vision, please.'

The squirrel pressed a button on the side of the goggles. Vetman peered closer and sighed. 'It's worse than I thought. The blood supply has been cut off for too long. There's no way to save the legs – they're already gangrenous.'

'What does that mean?' asked Imogen.

'It means these legs will have to go,' said Vetman.

'No!' said Imogen, tears springing up into her eyes. 'Is there nothing you can do?'

Chapter 6

On instruction from Vetman, the squirrel lifted the glasses up to his forehead and he looked into Imogen's eyes. His eyes were wet too, and she knew he was feeling just as bad as she was. 'There are many things we *could* do,' said Vetman softly. 'The question is, what's for the best – what's ethically the right thing to do? The poor hog must have been in terrible pain. But without his legs, he won't survive.'

The sadness in Imogen's chest turned to anger. 'But we came all the way here! The squirrel brought us. We can't just let him die!'

Vetman gazed around the bunker and his eyes widened as they settled on one corner, in which lay a mound of old appliances like washing machines, fridges and TV sets.

Then he leaned across the operating table and whispered to the monkey. He, in turn, jumped along the elephant's trunk and lifted his ear, grunting a few sounds into it. Together with the platypus and several other animals, they set to work lifting items out of the way, until they found an ancient vacuum cleaner.

'What are they doing?' asked Imogen.

'Looking for a solution,' said Vetman.

'But how do they understand you?' pressed Findlay. 'And each other.'

'Understanding is about trust,' said Vetman. 'The language is not important.'

'So you speak Monkey?' said Findlay.

Vetman's eyebrows rose. 'Animals have all kinds of different languages, just like people from different countries. They often understand each other well enough, just like you studying a foreign language for a while. I struggle sometimes myself with chameleon dragons, for example, but mostly I understand them and they understand me.'

The alligator cracked open the vacuum cleaner with his teeth, and the parrot bent over and began to saw at the insides with her razor-sharp chromium beak.

Then the monkey picked out two small springs and rubbed the rust off on the platypus's cheese-grater belly. Last of all, the elephant squirted them clean with some fluid from his trunk. The budgies, each of which seemed to have tinfoil wings, then dropped the springs in the bowl of iodine disinfectant held by the guinea pigs. Imogen saw that Vetman had already amputated the hedgehog's legs below the knees. Before today, the sight would have frightened her beyond belief, but something about his calm presence drove away any fear.

'Drill, please, Findlay,' he said.

With his lips parted in wonder, Imogen's brother passed the drill to Vetman. The squirrel popped the goggles back down on Vetman's eyes, and Imogen guessed that the goggles not only saw the blood supply but also magnified what he was looking at, because she could hardly make out what he was doing at all, as he positioned the springs and took tiny screws from a tray. The springs fitted perfectly over the top of the broken shin bones just under the knees, where he screwed them in place using brackets. Finally, he stitched the wounds up with thread from the spool, now held by the tarantula. He stood back.

'That should do it,' he said. 'Ah, but there's one more thing!'

He ripped off his gown and then reached into a small concealed pocket in his surgical scrubs, gently taking out a tiny vial of sparkling crystals. They glinted in the light from the owl's eyes. He took off the cap and delicately sprinkled the silvery dust across the wound at the junction of the bone, skin and springs. It sparkled like liquid starlight, like something not of this world.

'What's that?' asked Imogen. 'Is it to stop infection?'

'Oh, that, and more,' said Vetman. 'Much, much, more. This dust was harvested from the very beginnings of time and space. A most precious commodity. The animals call it Bionic Dust.'

Imogen wanted to ask more, but Vetman was talking to the animals again. The tarantula removed the mask from the hedgehog's face, and the parrot carried the drapes away and dropped them into a bin. Everyone stood back. Slowly, the patient's nose twitched and he began to move. Imogen couldn't imagine what he would make of the strange new appendages in place of his legs, but after a few wobbling steps he seemed to get the hang of it, bobbing up and down. He turned to look at the animals surrounding the operating table and at Imogen and Findlay, giving a series of squeaks.

'He says "thank you",' said Vetman. 'Now, you go steady, my little friend. Take your painkillers. No need to rush things.'

Laughter escaped Imogen's lips, as all her worries seeped away in a rush. She couldn't believe what she was seeing. The hedgehog seemed to be enjoying himself, jumping higher and higher. Imogen caught

her breath as he fell off the
edge of the table, but to
her astonishment the spiky
creature simply bounced
across the floor.

'You fixed him with bits from
an old vacuum cleaner!' said Findlay.

'That's what we do here,' said
Vetman. 'Most of the bionic parts are
recycled from stuff that was thrown
away or rejected, just like all of these poor
animals were discarded as useless. You know, we throw
away the best things in life and don't realise until
they're gone. And now look . . . they have hope and
they have love. You see, everything is possible, when
it's the right thing to do.'

The elephant gave a trumpet, and the monkey
hooted. The parrot flapped her wings and squawked.
All of the animals across the bunker joined in the

chorus of celebration. Imogen put her arm around her brother and for once he didn't pull away. He was grinning from ear to ear.

'We did it!' Imogen said. 'A miraculous bionic hedgehog!'

The Man With No Name

On the other side of the village, at the end of a lane where no one ever ventured, stood a large tree that hadn't borne leaves or blossom for many years. No birds sang in its branches. Its bare and knotted roots clung to the earth like grizzled fingers holding on for dear life. Some said lightning had struck the tree, but this wasn't true. The poison that stripped the branches bare came from deep inside. Hidden out of sight, disguised by the patterns in the bark, was a wooden door. It led downwards, into a cavern deep underground, lit only by the thin shafts of light that crept through the roots of the tree. Here lived the Man With No Name.

He snorted awake in the half-haze of dawn. From his mouth came an angry growl which echoed around the walls of his den. Black eyes opened in his scrunched-up face and took in the dank and mouldy walls. His bed was a congealed mess of old sackcloth and animal skin. He swung his legs off the stinking furs and lit a greasy oil lamp. Faint streaks of light picked out the skeleton heads of dead animals that hung from the ceiling like decorations. The earth and stone walls around him dripped with damp, like the sweat of nightmares, between the empty-eyed heads of a lion, a tiger, a rhinoceros and even a sloth.

He cleared his throat and spat out a ball of phlegm into the corner of the room.

It was time to get to work.

Carrying the lamp, he moved across the chamber barefoot, snagging his curled-up gnarly toenails on the animal skins and feathers strewn all over the grimy floor. There was skin and hair of a dozen or more animals sewn together – wool from a sheep, hair from a goat, tufts from a badger and some fleece from a stoat, ears from a hare and even some scales from a crocodile woven in there. He reached the crusty curtain hanging from iron hooks and drew it aside. As he did, birds trapped in cages on the other side cawed nervously. Others, too sick to make much sound at all, pressed themselves against the bars pitifully. The Man With No Name clapped his hands together as he surveyed his experiments. Several large canisters stood over a brazier, with pipes and a complicated array of taps and dials leading off and up the walls that finally entered a tank of glass and tarnished metal.

The man lit the burner flames and the stench of gas filled the air, making the birds in the cages flap and panic.

'Shut up!' yelled the Man With No Name. The birds obeyed. He pulled a large rubber mask over his head, tucked in his wispy strands of long knotted hair and attached a breathing tube to his mouth. He grizzled and grumbled as he pulled on an apron and long plastic gloves.

Next he took out his purchases from the trip to town – disinfectant, bleach, acidic cleaner and garden fertiliser, bought in bulk. He had been experimenting for months and knew his mixture was nearly perfect. He poured some into the different canisters over the flames, and measured others into the various tanks. He adjusted the pressure dials and the temperatures. All the time, as he worked, he sang in a tuneless voice.

'I hate you. I hate you. I hate you all. Your smiles and your laughter I'll turn to a bawl. I hate all you children and all of the animals that bring you joy. I think you're all stupid and I think you're all vile. Your smiles and your laughter I intend to destroy. It's Christmastime . . . the perfect time for my magnificent crime . . . Hah, hah!'

Soon the pots were simmering and the air was filled

with noxious fumes. Tendrils of foul smoke rose up through the pipes from the bubbling vats, collecting and mingling. The Man With No Name continued to mutter to himself.

'I hate you. I hate you. I hate the dogs and the cats and I hate all of the children who hug and kiss their horrible little noses. With these doses, I will wipe the smile right off your faces. I hate you, I hate you, I hate you all and soon I'll bring tears to all happy places . . .'

As the chemicals mingled, a steady stream of drips fell in the glass flask beneath one big bubbling apparatus. The liquid was clear, and to an untrained eye it might have looked like water. It was anything but.

The Man With No Name watched the drops fall with a gleam in his eye and a swell of pride in his black heart. It was almost done.

Leaving the concoction brewing and the birds

cowering in their cages, he ripped off the mask and made his way to what could only have been his study, though it was more like a hovel, where piles of dusty papers and books lay in disarray across tables and the floor. He sat down, breathing heavily, on a huge chair shaped like a throne, made from the bones of animals and covered with hides. The heads of dead birds stared from pillars on the upright back and the heads of dead foxes poked up from the armrests where he laid his big shovel-like hands beside him. The chair creaked under his great weight.

His eyes travelled around the room. Along the wall opposite, lined up along a tilting shelf, were his aerial troops . . . his flying soldiers. These were birds too, but completely lifeless. They were big black mechanical crows, with their beady red eyes staring and empty. The Man With No Name grinned, baring rotten stumps of teeth, jutting out like jagged rocks in his mouth. No one could know what he was planning, and no one could stop him. The whole country was preparing for Christmas – hanging their mistletoe, decorating their trees, wrapping their presents. Wrapped up themselves in their joy, they were blind to what was coming.

His eyes moved to the table at his side, where a small photo stood in a frame. It showed a small boy, his smile was beaming, his arms wrapped around the neck of a giant fluffy Newfoundland dog with a huge kind face and droopy eyes. The Man With No Name bit his lip, fighting back the tears that threatened to roll over his pitted cheeks and his three bristly chins. He took the photo in a shovel hand and laid it flat so he couldn't see it any more. That boy was in the past. He'd had a name, and love in his heart.

The man on his throne had neither.

He brimmed with hate. It grew inside him, leaking from his pores and tingling to his fingertips.

Almost done. A day or two more and he'd have enough of the poison to put his plan into action. But he still had to test it properly, and for that the birds wouldn't do. He needed something bigger, and he knew just where to get such a victim.

Chapter 7

It was only when Imogen checked her watch that she realised how long they'd been in the bunker. She'd been enchanted as the animals cleared up the operating table, working together in perfect harmony.

'We've got to get going!' she said.

'Do we have to?' moaned Findlay. He was enjoying a ride on the alligator's back.

'It's nearly four o'clock in the morning!' said Imogen. She looked around but couldn't see Vetman. After a brief search, she located him in an alcove. The hedgehog, resting on a shelf, seemed to be squeaking directly into his ear.

'A motorbike, you say?' Vetman was responding.

The hedgehog shuddered and made a clicking sound.

Vetman rubbed his stubbled chin, deep in thought. 'I don't like the sound of that at all.'

'Is something wrong?' asked Imogen.

Vetman looked up with a haunted expression. 'Our little friend was just telling me how he came about his injuries. He says a man deliberately ran over him.'

'That's horrible!' said Imogen. 'Who would be so cruel?'

Vetman opened his mouth as if about to say something, then stopped himself. 'You don't have to go far in our world to find cruelty,' he said.

Imogen knew that was true. She saw it everywhere. In the bullies in the playground at school, in the news, and occasionally even at Pet Haven, in the poor dogs and cats who'd been mistreated.

Vetman put his hand on her shoulder. 'The important

thing, my dear, is to make sure the good overwhelms the bad,' he said. 'Like you have tonight.'

'I'm afraid we have to go home now,' she said.

'Of course you do,' said Vetman, clambering stiffly to his feet. He walked them back to the elevator platform and the squirrel pulled a lever in the rock. They rose, and the bionic bunker shrank below them, the incredible creatures disappearing from view. Soon the cottage appeared above and they were standing in the entrance hall once more. There was nothing that would have given any clue as to the miracle workshop far below.

'Can we come back?' said Imogen. The words left her mouth before she'd really had time to consider them.

Vetman turned his kind gaze on her and her brother as the platform settled into place at the far end of the hall. He looked tired, she thought. Almost shrunken.

'Maybe one day,' he said. 'But not straight away.'

His face was suddenly serious. 'There are other matters I must attend to.'

'We can help!' said Findlay eagerly.

Vetman shook his head sadly. 'I'm afraid not. Not with this. It might be dangerous.'

'Is it something to do with the man on the motorbike?' asked Imogen.

Vetman's eyebrows rose. 'You're a clever girl, Imogen. And a good person. But, please, for your own safety, don't ask me more. And as I said before, you mustn't tell anyone I'm here. People just don't understand. They'd put a stop to all of this.'

She desperately wanted to ask more but managed to hold her tongue. The squirrel bounced up on to Vetman's shoulder, the bristles of her tail sparkling.

'Our friend here will guide you back home,' he said. 'Thank you, Imogen and Findlay, for all you've done.'

'But we barely did anything,' she said.

'Oh, but you did *the most* extraordinary thing,' said

Vetman. 'If it weren't for your kindness, the hedgehog would not have survived.'

That was true, Imogen supposed. She felt a flush of pride on her cheeks. Vetman held out his hand. 'Safe travels, both of you.'

Without thinking, Imogen rushed forward and wrapped her arms around him. Vetman hugged her back. Findlay joined the embrace too.

After they broke apart, Imogen and her brother followed the squirrel to the edge of the clearing. Though it was still cold, the snow crunching underfoot, the warmth in her heart made her limbs tingle. Just before they entered the trees, she looked back and saw Vetman was still standing in the doorway, a little bit hunched. She wondered if she'd ever see him again.

* * *

The journey home seemed quick. They recovered their bikes and followed the squirrel through the deserted streets until they arrived back in their own road. To Imogen's surprise, there were lights on in many of the houses, even though it was way too early for people to be up. And as they reached their own home, she saw why.

'Oh no,' said Imogen.

Lights were on in all the windows of their house, and the front door was open. Mum stood there in her dressing gown with a phone in one hand, surrounded by several of their neighbours. When she saw them, her hand went to her mouth and she rushed out.

Imogen and her brother climbed off their bikes, just in time for their mum to wrap them in her embrace. It was a hug of love but also deep concern.

'Where have you *been*?' she said.

Imogen hardly knew what to say, but when Mum released them again she saw anger on her tear-stained face.

'We took the hedgehog to a vet in the forest,' blurted

Findlay, 'and he's got this bionic bunker where he fixes all the animals. There's an elephant and an alligator and—'

'Shut up!' hissed Imogen, panicking.

'What on earth are you talking about?' asked their mum as she hurried them back into the house.

'We followed a squirrel with a tail made from a bristly brush,' said Findlay. He turned and pointed back into the street. 'She's right there . . .'

But she wasn't. The squirrel had vanished.

Their mum said thank you to the neighbours, who all looked relieved, if confused, as they drifted back to their beds.

Once the front door was closed, Imogen's mum took her by the shoulders. 'Immy, I don't know what you've been filling his head with, but you're supposed to be the responsible one! How could you do this? It's freezing out there!'

Imogen looked at her brother, stuck for words.

'I got half the neighbours up. I was about to call the police!' said Mum. 'Tell me, where were you?'

Imogen wanted to. She really did. She wanted to tell her mum all about the wonderful, amazing things they'd seen in the forest. About Vetman, and the animals, and the operation. She wanted to lead her mum there right then, but she couldn't break her promise to Vetman. He had put his trust in her.

'We just . . . went for a bike ride,' she said quietly. 'It was a starry night and I missed Daddy – and the camping and stuff – so I went for a ride to clear my head. Findlay wanted to come too. He couldn't sleep either.'

Her mum's features softened a bit at the mention of their father, but she was still very upset. 'I don't know what to say. Both of you need to go to bed and we'll discuss this in the morning. Upstairs. Now.'

Imogen took off her boots and coat, and traipsed up the stairs behind Findlay.

But as she lay under her duvet, she couldn't stop her mind racing. After a few minutes she looked across to her brother's bed.

'Are you still awake?' she asked.

'Yeah,' he said sleepily.

'Did all that just happen?'

'I think so,' he said.

It must have then. Two people couldn't imagine the same fantasy.

'Then we can't tell anyone at all – absolutely nobody,'

she said. 'It's got to be our secret.'

She wasn't sure if Findlay had heard her. His breathing was soft and slow. He'd only told Mum because she was so worried about them. And it wasn't like she'd ever believe it. Outside, through the window, clouds had covered the stars. Imogen closed her eyes, images of the bionic bunker and Vetman and all the bionic animals filling her head.

Chapter 8

Next day Mum was in a *bad* mood as she drove Imogen to Pet Haven. She'd barely spoken all morning, other than to mutter how disappointed she was. Imogen knew there was nothing she could do or say to make things better, and she was glad Findlay didn't try either. He seemed to know it was best to keep quiet. What made it worse still was that Imogen had been planning to bring up the subject of adopting Pirate. But that dream seemed more distant than ever. There was no way Mum would say yes now.

As they pulled up at the sanctuary, Mum put her hand across and laid it on Imogen's knee. Imogen thought she was going to say something else about being a responsible big sister, but it wasn't that.

'I'm going to nip to see Dad later – if you fancy it.'

Imogen stiffened in her seat. 'No, thanks,' she said quickly.

'Come on,' said Findlay from the back. 'It's just a grave.'

'Maybe next time,' she said, getting out so she didn't have to carry on the conversation.

'OK, sweetheart,' said Mum softly. 'I'll pick you up later.'

Imogen walked across to the front doors. Findlay had no problem at all with the weekly trips to the cemetery, and Imogen wasn't sure exactly why she was so terrified of joining them. It wasn't even that the place was spooky or anything. Like her brother said, it was just a grave, after all. But the one time she had been there, after the funeral, it had felt all wrong to see his headstone lost among all the others. As though he wasn't special at all, and the world was ready to forget about him. All his life was reduced to just a dash between two dates: when he was born and when he died. She'd wanted to scream at everyone that his life was more than that – he was more than just a dash.

She'd come close to going in a couple of times since, but as they'd approached the cemetery gates, a sensation had crept over her, like the noise of a raging waterfall getting louder and louder until it was pounding in her ears. It felt like it was pushing her back with an invisible force. It was silly, really. If her little brother could manage it, there was no reason she shouldn't.

She'd almost reached the door of the sanctuary when it burst open. A very large man in dark clothing entirely filled the doorway. He paused a moment before barging past her, as if he hadn't even noticed her, or didn't care. The first thing that struck her was his smell, like the contents of a bin left out in the sun. She barely saw his face, because it was concealed in shadow under

the wide-brimmed hat pulled low over his head. As he swept past her, a long tatty coat trailing behind him, she noticed he was carrying something, covered up under the edge of his coat.

His battered boots with big metal caps clopped across the car park. When he reached a rusty motorbike with a bird skeleton painted on the chassis, he produced a cat crate from beneath his coat, which he perched roughly behind the handlebars over the fuel tank. As he swung himself into the saddle, a distressed miaow came from the crate. Imogen was about to go and tell him he should be more careful, but she was distracted by him taking off his hat, revealing lank strands of hair like seaweed. He pulled on a helmet, kicked out the bike stand and revved the engine. Smoke coughed from the exhaust and he roared away. As he swept off, Imogen thought she caught a glimpse of a terrified pair of eyes from inside the crate.

For a moment, she stood there, racking her brains.

Had she seen the man before somewhere? No one had ever come to the sanctuary on a motorbike, and most new guardians were generally *a lot* gentler with their new animal friends. It made her think of something Vetman had said. Hadn't the hedgehog been hit by a motorbike? It could be a coincidence, but . . .

Troubled, Imogen walked inside. Ciara looked up from the front desk, smiling.

'Good morning, Immy! Gosh – you look tired! Late night?'

'A bit,' said Imogen. 'Who was that man?'

'His name was Mr Byrne,' said Ciara. 'He took a fancy to Rupert the old tabby. Sweet, really.'

'He didn't look very nice,' said Imogen. 'Or smell nice, for that matter.'

'A bit like Rupert then,' laughed Ciara. 'I didn't think he'd ever find a home.'

Imogen couldn't deny that. Rupert had been at the

sanctuary for almost two years, the longest feline resident.

'He showed me a picture of him and his dear mother at their beautiful farmhouse,' Ciara went on. 'Rupert will have a grand time wandering the farmyard and I'm sure he'll be looked after really well.'

'Has he had cats before?' asked Imogen doubtfully.

'Oh yes,' said Ciara. 'And dogs. His references all checked out. I kind of remembered him too, from years and years ago. He and his mum have always rescued strays. In fact, they took one when I first started this place – a beautiful Newfoundland, I think it was! Ah well, we're all getting old now, I suppose. He's not looking the best himself these days – he looked younger in the picture, but I suppose it was taken a few years ago – and it just shows, you can't judge a book by its cover. Now, would you mind watching the desk while I do a food stocktake?'

Imogen said that was fine and watched Ciara go.

Whether it was the smell of the strange man still in the air or just the menace of his presence lingering, she couldn't shake off the queasy feeling in her stomach.

She looked at the logbook on the counter, where all the new adopters were recorded. His name was on the open page.

Mr T. Byrne, Cross Farm, Quiet Lane.

Imogen knew of this road, but she couldn't picture any farm out that way. She tried to tell herself it was fine. Ciara would never let an animal go to a home she thought was unsafe. Every potential guardian was well vetted beforehand. But there was something about the man that didn't sit right with Imogen. The way he'd thrown the crate across the saddle said he was no animal lover. Quite the opposite, in fact. He'd acted exactly like the sort of man who might run over a hedgehog. And if he *was* that man, there was no saying what he'd do to poor old Rupert.

Chapter 9

Imogen couldn't concentrate on her work at the sanctuary at all. She knew that she was tired and more than a bit stressed, but most of all she couldn't get the motorbike man out of her head. She was worried for Rupert and there was only one person she could think of who might be able to help. She accidentally fed cat food to the first two dogs before realising her mistake when Pirate – the third in line – sniffed at his bowl with suspicion. He looked up at her with his big eyes behind his pirate patch, as if he knew something else much more important was wrong. He reached up his paw and placed it on Imogen's knee as she knelt down beside him. She stooped, wrapped her arms around his neck and hugged him tightly as he licked her face. Pirate always knew when Imogen needed some love.

'Are you OK?' asked Ciara, who found her replacing the bowls.

'Not really,' Imogen replied. She'd already decided what she had to do. 'I think I'm coming down with something.'

'Want me to ring your mum?'

That wouldn't work, so she quickly thought up an excuse.

'No. It's OK – I'll walk home.'

'I don't think that's a good idea,' said Ciara. 'Not if you're unwell.' She pulled out a phone and began to dial.

'Don't,' said Imogen. 'She'll be at the cemetery. With Findlay. I don't want to disturb them. Honestly, I'm fine to walk.'

Ciara looked uncertain, but then nodded. 'Call me when you're safely home,' she said.

Imogen promised she would, then said goodbye to Pirate. 'I'll be back tomorrow,' she said, scratching him behind the ears. He gazed after her with a concerned look in his eyes.

But she didn't go home. Instead, she walked back to the same gap in the hedge they'd been led to by the squirrel the night before. It wasn't hard to follow the tracks of their bikes, and it was reassuring to know for certain that none of it had been a dream. At the forest edge, which was much less spooky in the daytime, she didn't hesitate. She still wasn't sure if this was all a waste of time, but better safe than sorry.

And soon enough, she came to the clearing, and to Vetman's cottage. It was unmistakably the same place, but *something* was different. Hadn't the chimney been at the other end of the roof? And hadn't there been three steps leading up to the front door where now there were only two? Imogen figured she was mistaken. Houses didn't change shape over night. She knocked at the door and waited. No one came, so she knocked again, harder this time, thumping the door with her fist. Still there was no sound from the other side. Perhaps he was out. Or maybe he was in his bunker, hard at work, and simply couldn't hear.

She tried the door handle and to her surprise it was unlocked. She entered.

'Hello?' she called.

No answer. She thought about turning round and leaving. Barging into people's homes uninvited wasn't something Imogen would normally have done. The polite and normal thing would have been to wait by the door for him to return.

But there was nothing normal about the last twenty-four hours. Or about the man on the motorbike – Mr Byrne. If that was even his real name.

She went inside and the hall was longer than she

had remembered, but she finally came to the lever on the wall. She pulled it. After a few second of rattling and clunking, the floor began to descend, carrying her with it.

The bionic bunker was quiet, laid out exactly as they'd left it the night before, but with no animals in sight. The alligator pool was still, and no birds fluttered in the air. As the platform touched down, Imogen stepped off. 'Hello?' Her voice echoed through the cavernous space.

Where *was* everyone?

Then she heard a faint tapping sound at her feet. It was the tarantula, scuttling across the hard floor. She stopped briefly, turning her eyes on Imogen, then continued on her path towards an archway in a darkened alcove at the rear of the bunker. Imogen followed, hurrying to keep up. She passed under the arch and into a tunnel made of some kind of metal that glowed with dim lights embedded in the walls.

This part of the bunker felt different – somehow space-age and ancient at the same time. The air was cooler and the walls were marked with rows and rows of engravings in neat lines. She thought they looked like the pictures of hieroglyphs she'd seen in books about Ancient Egypt at school – strange human-animal hybrids mixed with symbols she couldn't understand.

Then she heard noises. Animals, all baying and moaning and croaking softly. As she crept onwards, the sounds grew until she found herself looking down into a small circular burrow nestled in the rocks among the roots of old trees. The bionic animals were all here – the elephant with his trunk lowered, the tortoise resting on her hind legs, the birds perched on a rail nearby, the monkey hanging from the ceiling. All were looking down, towards an extraordinary sight in a hollowed-out area in the middle. There was a cocoon shaped like a large cradle, with sides that looked like the huge curled petals of an opalescent flower on the

end of a pulsing blue stem, which acted like a pedestal to suspend it somehow, just above the ground. Vetman lay in the centre of this strange cradle, like a pea in a pod, a delicate creature cupped in a shell. His scrub-top with the 'V M' letters on it was pulled up, revealing his chest. There, right over his heart, his skin was marked with azure swirls, like a tattoo, but the image seemed to be alive, the colours ebbing and flowing, throbbing in time with the pulsing of the stem.

Imogen moved closer, trying to work out what she was looking at. It seemed that whatever the cradle was, it was feeding him, bonding with him somehow. Vetman's eyes were closed, but his eyelids flickered and his features twitched as if he was dreaming. Around the cocoon in this chamber she saw there was some kind of high-tech laboratory, even more advanced and other-worldly than the bionic bunker. It was full of bleeping lights, vials of coloured, iridescent liquids, shining fabric and metal hanging in glowing orbs or giant glass tubes nestled in recesses in the walls – and all manner of whirring machines and contraptions. There were banks of monitors too, with views of every nook and cranny of the bionic bunker from the cocoon. It was like a control centre of some sort.

Suddenly Vetman's eyes opened, as green as sunlight glowing through summer leaves. They fixed on her. She backed away, her heart skipping a beat. In the same moment, the animals turned towards her as well. The elephant let out an irritated trumpet as if she shouldn't be there, and the guinea pigs swarmed around her feet. Vetman scrambled off the cradle.

She tried to turn to leave, but a rushing sound filled her ears and she whirled around to see the tortoise blocking her path, hovering in mid-air. She realised the handles of the wheelbarrow contained tiny jets, filled with fire, that kept the tortoise aloft. The alligator slithered up alongside, placing his bulk between

Imogen and the way out. Just as she was wondering if she was in danger, Vetman appeared too, still pulling down his scrub-top over his chest.

'I'm sorry!' Imogen said. 'I didn't mean to intrude.'

But he looked more embarrassed than angry. 'No, it's quite all right,' he said. 'I . . . I simply wasn't expecting visitors.'

'I knocked,' she explained. 'No one came, but I thought . . . Well, I needed to find you. It might be nothing . . .'

'Take your time,' said Vetman, looking around at all the animals as if to reassure them that everything was all right. 'We're all friends here.'

So Imogen explained what had happened at Pet Haven. She tried to relate it in a calm way, but she found her fears rising as she described the man on the motorbike – the way he moved and the way he smelled, and the sinister aura that lingered in his wake. She expected Vetman to dismiss her worries, but the effect was quite the opposite. A deep frown etched his forehead.

'A cat, you say?' he muttered.

'An old, sweet-natured cat,' said Imogen.

Vetman sighed. 'Hmm . . . a couple of months ago my animal friends brought reports of a few sickly cats in the area being taken to local vets. They brought it to my attention because I treated one myself – a poor starving stray. I'm sorry to say, he was too far gone for me to save. Before he died, he spoke to me of a man who offered him food. He thought the man was being kind, but he wasn't. It was bad food – and it killed him. At the time I thought it must be someone being stupid, and that the food was rotten, but I wonder . . .'

'You think he's poisoning them?' cried Imogen.

'It's possible,' murmured Vetman.

'Then we have to stop him!' she replied.

'We'd have to find him first,' said Vetman. 'That won't be easy.'

'Yes it will!' said Imogen, and she told Vetman the man's address. 'We should go there, right now. Rupert might be in terrible danger.'

Vetman turned away and ran a hand through his hair. 'No,' he said. 'This is not a job for a human girl.'

Imogen shook her head. 'Why do you keep calling me that?' she said. 'You're a human too.'

Vetman faced her again, his expression grave. 'You are the best of them,' he said, 'but there's so much you don't know. I cannot risk harm coming to you. Thank you for bringing me this information but I will handle the next step alone.'

Imogen stood her ground. 'No, you won't,' she said fiercely.

Vetman looked shocked. 'You don't understand.'

Imogen folded her arms. 'No, *you* don't understand. Rupert came from Pet Haven. That means he's *my* responsibility. I'm going to Cross Farm, whether you like it or not.'

Chapter 9

Behind her, the monkey let out a series of chittering calls. Vetman's eyes widened and he nodded wearily. 'She certainly is,' he said, before looking at her sternly. 'Imogen, leave this to me, please. After dark, I'll pay Cross Farm a visit and see what I can learn about this Mr Byrne. It's not a place for a young girl.'

Imogen hung her head. 'I'm not scared,' she mumbled.

Vetman's voice softened. 'Imogen, I know you're not,' he said. 'That's the problem. Maybe you should be.'

The Man With No Name

In the corner of the den, the old cat gave out a frightened miaow from his crate.

'Quiet!' bellowed the Man With No Name, without turning round. Flecks of spittle hit the monitor in front of him. It showed the girl from the animal sanctuary. His coal-black eyes squinted and his spiky chins quivered. He didn't know her name, but he didn't like her face. She was too clever, too young and too full of hope and love. He didn't like the face of any child – but especially not a child like that.

And he certainly didn't like the way she'd looked at him earlier.

He pressed a button to make the footage speed up. The girl had left the sanctuary in a hurry, then run practically all the way to the forest at the edge of town. His eyes in the sky had lost her in the trees, but then spotted her once more as she reached a strange cottage in the clearing. From the way she approached, he didn't think it was *her* house, but whose could it be?

He turned his head, and his eyes travelled to a map hanging on the bare earth wall. It had taken two years to put together his targets and each was marked with a red cross. But that wasn't all. He knew more than their locations. Much more. He'd investigated the exact layout of each building well. The doors and windows, numbers of staff and when they clocked on and off, security arrangements, when the gates opened to let in trucks, where the ingredients were unloaded and stored. His plans were perfect, and it would take more than a little girl to stop him now. He couldn't wait to see her face wet with tears, and all the joy sucked from her hopeful features.

The Man With No Name hummed and whistled an ominous tune to himself as he pottered between vials of steaming liquid and tanks of bubbling chemicals. 'Ha-ha, tee-hee, I'm the man with a plan, don't ya see, and there's nobody going to outwit me. I spread deathly dread and I couldn't care less, cos I'm a man with a plan, and my plan is the best. Woe is me, woe is me, I work all night as I plan their plight and I am the king of misery – so I'll have my revenge, they will see! Hah, hah!'

The cat miaowed again, pawing at the bars of his prison. Perhaps old Rufus, or whatever his name was, wanted a cuddle or a stroke. The very thought made him feel sick. He'd just as soon plunge his hands into flames as give comfort to a cat.

'You'll get no love from me,' said the Man With No Name. 'I've got something else planned for you.

Something quite, quite beautiful.'

He stood up, sending a waft of his vegetable stench across the den. The cat flinched.

The man strode over to the cage and unfastened the door. Inside, the cat arched his spine in fear and hissed. He reached inside, and, though Rupert clawed, the man's skin was as thick as hardened leather and he felt nothing. He grabbed Rupert behind his ears and dragged him out. He lifted the feline to face him and smiled. 'Feeding time for you,' he said. 'One more test. Then everything will be well and truly ready.'

Chapter 10

Imogen had been lying to Vetman. She *was* scared.

But that wasn't going to stop her going to Cross Farm.

Every little fear faced . . . as her dad used to say.

It was close to midnight, and in the quiet of her bedroom she rolled up several bundles of clothes and put them under her duvet, to make it look like a body asleep beneath. If Mum looked in, which was unlikely, she'd hopefully be fooled. She'd had to pretend she was still feeling rotten after leaving Pet Haven earlier, and she felt guilty deceiving her mum. She seemed to be doing a lot of that recently, but what other choice was there? Like Vetman said, she only hoped she was doing it for the right reason.

She decided not to wake her brother. It was one thing to put herself in danger, but Findlay was still just a little kid. And she knew very well that Mum would never forgive her for taking him out at night again.

Imogen wouldn't forgive herself either, if something were to happen to Findlay. He looked so peaceful, fast asleep. When Dad had died, he'd woken almost every night with bad dreams, but they'd stopped now, thank goodness.

She wasn't going to make the same mistake as last time, and dressed in several layers, taking a woolly coat, scarf and gloves. Going along her street was too risky tonight, in case one of the nosy neighbours saw, so Imogen went out of the back door, down the garden and through the gap in the broken fence. She didn't look back as she entered the Wilderness. There were no trolls in here, of course, just tangled brambles and litter blown off the nearby road, but it was still scary to know she was entering a place strictly forbidden by both her parents. The night was cloudy – no constellations, no Canis Major, no Sirius. But up there, somewhere, Dad was watching. She wondered what he would make of her actions. Would he be proud of or angry at his little girl?

Imogen made her way between the looming, frozen trees, and in no time at all she'd reached the road. She hurried quickly along the edge until she saw the lights of the village behind her in the distance. Quiet Lane wasn't far – she'd checked the way on a map before she left – and it was easy to see how it had got its name. A dark and lonely track, with no lights and no cars and leading nowhere. A sign at the end read 'Private – No Access'. Imogen steeled her nerves and ignored it. She'd brought a torch with her, but didn't switch it on until she had to. It threw an arc of light ahead, and outside the hard edges of the beam the night was so dark there might have been nothing at all. She wished she had Findlay with her after all. Two people scared together was somehow better than one.

After a few hundred metres, the lane petered out, becoming a rough track, deep rutted and overgrown with weeds. She'd have guessed no one lived up this way at all.

But there, at last, was Cross Farm. Imogen swept the torch back and forth.

Ciara had said it was a beautiful location, and maybe it had been a *long* time ago. Now it was clearly abandoned – a tumbledown farmhouse surrounded by crumbling old machinery and a barn built of corrugated metal, which was rusty and dilapidated, with jagged bits of metal that looked like shark's teeth against the hazy night sky. An old gnarly tree draped over the rusty edges like clawing fingers. The windows were boarded up, some sprayed with graffiti.

There was no sign of life at all. She checked her watch. Half past twelve.

Chapter 10

Her hopes began to fade: no one lived here, that was clear. Mr Byrne – or whatever his real name was – must have simply given this address to disguise the real place he'd taken poor Rupert. Vetman had probably been here already and gone home. In which case, it would *definitely* be a good idea for her to leave too. He was right: this was no place for a twelve-year-old girl on her own.

But not yet.

Her feet carried her closer, through a leaning open gate and into the overgrown front garden of the farmhouse. She kept her torch on the old door, from which the paint was peeling, alert for any movement and ready to run if she had to.

A noise from overhead made her start, breath snagging in her lungs, and she turned the glare of the torch upwards, into the sky. Perhaps it had been a bird or a bat, but there was nothing there now. No stars tonight. No moon – just grey with ghostly smudges of cloud. As soon as she had started to breathe more easily and lowered the torch, she heard the sound again. It sounded like a boat's sail, whipped by a gusting wind. She flashed the torch wildly and it caught a shadow, moving too fast for her to keep up. And too big to be a bird of any kind. Her heart began to thump faster, blood fizzing in her legs. She took a step back and stumbled. The world tipped as she fell, and the torch flew from her hand. It landed with a crack and flickered out.

The darkness that swallowed her was absolute.

A wail escaped Imogen's lips, despite her efforts to be quiet. She scrambled over the ground on her hands and knees, searching for the torch. She found it and pressed the switch with a fumbling hand.

Nothing happened.

Then she heard the sound again – the *snick* of flapping material. It was closer now, swooping just overhead. She felt its breath in her hair.

'Hello?' she croaked.

Suddenly a light fixed her to the spot. She shielded

her eyes and squinted. On the gutter of the house stood the tawny owl with his great feathered ears, turning his head like a lighthouse guiding ships in a storm. Imogen grinned. 'Hey there!' she waved.

'Good evening, Imogen,' said a voice. 'I had a feeling you'd show up.'

Imogen spun around. For a moment she couldn't see anyone at all, but then, against the wall of the barn itself, a shape rippled. Imogen rubbed her eyes. From what had been old, rusty corrugated metal one moment emerged a rust-coloured figure in a strange bodysuit.

'Vetman!'

As he stepped forwards, she couldn't take her eyes off his clothing. It was like armour, with thousands of gleaming overlapping scales that seemed to change colour as he moved. Rusty like metal, grey and brown like a tree, green like a leaf and silver like snow – and all in half-darkness, as if it were a mirror reflecting his surroundings. On his head was a helmet of the same material, with a visor over his eyes and nose. He reached up to press a button on the side of the helmet and the visor shot up to reveal his face beneath. Gauntlets covered his hands, with an array of buttons of different colours on both wrists. He wore heavy-duty boots that trickled smoke from pipes on the sides.

Imogen was lost for words. 'Wh . . . Where . . .'

'Sorry I'm late,' said Vetman. 'We had a sick badger at the bunker. I came as soon as I could.'

Imogen gathered herself. She hadn't heard him approach at all. In fact, the shape she'd seen in the sky must have actually have been Vetman himself. The suit appeared to have webbing under his arms. Along each forearm was a small strip of white feathers sticking straight up, and there were three similar rows of them on the top of his helmet, forming a crest. There were also small quills sticking up from both shoulders, reinforcing his armour.

'Did you *fly* here?' she asked.

Vetman nodded. 'It seemed the quickest way.'

Not for the first time, Imogen wondered just who Vetman was. She couldn't forget the sight of him in the bunker, hooked up to that cradle machine, like it was feeding him somehow, or maybe delivering medicine. He seemed much more than a wacky scientist who cared about animals.

'Found anything yet?' he asked.

Imogen shook her head. 'My torch went out, but I don't think anyone lives here.'

From nowhere, the brush-tailed squirrel appeared on Vetman's shoulder and squeaked into his ear. His eyes narrowed. 'Is that right? Lead the way then.'

The owl swept off the roof to light their way, and Imogen followed Vetman and the squirrel round to the side of the old house. Imogen couldn't take her eyes off Vetman's clothing. Though it had looked reptilian at first, she saw there were more feathers interlaced among the locking plates. The whole thing looked somehow tough but lightweight and flexible too, like no material she'd ever seen. And now that she was walking behind him, she could see that there were grooves in the back of the suit from which she could glimpse the very tips of what looked like wings protruding.

They reached a patch of derelict garden, with an old child's swing leaning to one side. The owl took up a new perch on the branch of a dead tree with a split trunk that had maybe been struck by lightning in the distant past. The squirrel was standing on top of what looked like a small grave headstone, and the owl's light picked up engraved letters.

'What's this then?' said Vetman.

Imogen peered closer and read the words in her head.

To our beloved Shep. May you run for ever in the stars.

'Who's Shep?' she muttered, glancing across at Vetman.

Confusion creased his eyes. He tugged off one of the gauntlets and reached towards the cold stone with his bare fingers, stroking the letters. He flinched, as though in pain.

'You poor, poor man,' he said.

'Shep's a man?' asked Imogen.

Vetman pulled back his hand and gave a deep sigh. He shook his head sadly. 'No, but—'

A deep growl split the silence, like a huge beast clearing its throat. Startled, the owl took flight and everything was flashing light and shadow as she rose into the sky. Vetman's visor slotted back into place automatically and his suit rippled as he dropped into a crouch, scanning every direction. It took Imogen a moment to pick up where the sound was coming from.

The tree!

A light appeared in the split in the trunk, growing bigger by the second, until, to her astonishment, a motorbike burst forth from within. In the saddle sat the man from Pet Haven. He wore no helmet, so his knotted greasy hair whipped around his shoulders. His face was set in a grimace, his deep-set black eyes boring into the darkness. His massive knobbly knuckles gripped the handlebars and his knees stuck out from both sides. He reminded Imogen of a giant squatting spider. The engine rose in pitch as the bike swept straight towards Vetman.

With a single, impossible bound, Imogen's companion shot vertically into the air, grabbing hold of a branch above and dangling as the motorbike swept past. The man who called himself Mr Byrne swung the bike around, throwing up an arc of mud from the spinning tyres. He aimed the wheels at Imogen.

'You won't stop me!' he shouted. With a twist of the throttle, he roared towards her.

'No!' cried Vetman. He flipped upside down on the branch, so he was dangling by his legs, and reached out his arms to Imogen. 'Jump!' he said.

Imogen leapt as high as she could, but Vetman's fingers were just out of reach and she fell back to the ground. The glare of the bike's headlight pinned her to the spot, and she knew there was nowhere to go.

She closed her eyes and braced herself for the impact.

Chapter 11

Thump!

She found herself tumbling, hit from the side by an unknown force. And when she rolled over and saw who was on top of her, she couldn't believe her eyes.

'Findlay!'

He looked terrified, and they both stared after the motorbike as it surged away down the track, its rear light like an angry red eye. Vetman landed at their side as lightly as a gymnast.

'Are you both all right?'

Imogen was more worried about her brother as she sat up. 'How did you find me?'

'I followed you,' he said, eyes gleaming.

'All the way?' gasped Imogen. 'Through the Wilderness? Along the road? Are you mad? You could've been . . .'

She grabbed him and pulled him towards her in an embrace. He fought and squirmed, but she held him tightly. She squeezed until the images of what might have happened left her head.

'Why did you go without me?' he said angrily, but muffled, as she held him close into her shoulder.

'I didn't want you to get hurt!' said Imogen. 'You're only eight!'

He managed to push her off. There were tears on his cheeks, but his eyes were full of fury. 'And you're only twelve,' he said. 'And that man nearly ran you over! How d'you think Mum would feel if you died?'

He was shouting, on the verge of tears. Imogen didn't have an answer for that. Or for anything that was happening.

Vetman was standing over them, the squirrel back on his shoulder, his face full of worry. 'Your brother is right, Imogen,' he said. 'I should never have let you come here.'

'You didn't have a choice, remember,' said Imogen.

The owl was directing his light into the tree from which the motorbike had emerged. Imogen saw past the split in the bark, to what appeared to be a tunnel leading downwards. She picked herself up.

'What's down there?' mumbled Findlay. His small hand found hers and squeezed.

'Let me go first,' said Vetman.

Imogen didn't argue, and they followed their companion towards the gnarly tree. The owl hopped at their side, lighting the way. A sloping passage, the walls wet and lined with roots, descended into the ground. It led perhaps twenty metres until it levelled out into an underground cavern. The first thing Imogen noticed was the smell – a rotten-vegetable tang that turned her stomach. It reminded her of the time she'd left a banana in her lunchbox at school over the holidays. Oil lamps smoked and filled the cavern with soft light – clearly Mr Byrne had left in a hurry – and the owl switched off his guiding beam. The ceiling was uneven and crumbling, with more roots and rocks sticking through, but the floor was hard-packed earth, scattered here and there with black feathers. Several curtains hung down, separating the space into different rooms. The three companions walked through slowly, pushing the grimy drapes aside.

The first part looked like a bedroom of some sort. There was an old couch, lined with stinking animal furs and mouldy old blankets. On a shelf, and hanging from the roof on twines, spinning slowly on currents of air, were the skulls of various animals, large and small, from delicate birds to what might have been sheep or goats, or perhaps even dogs and cats. Their eye sockets watched as Imogen and the others walked beneath. She didn't want to think how the poor creatures had met their ends.

'This place is gross!' said Findlay. 'Who'd want to live here?'

The next room resembled a ramshackle chemistry lab. It seemed the exact opposite of the bionic bunker, with everything filthy and dusty and rusting. Broken glass littered the ground, and dented pipes sprouted from various tanks, winding their way across the walls. Puddles of sludge and strange-coloured stains covered the workbench.

'What's he up to?' she muttered.

Vetman joined her, his eyes travelling over the apparatus. He picked up a container and sniffed, his features screwing up.

'Poison?' said Imogen, recalling Vetman's tales of poorly cats and bad food.

'I expect so,' said Vetman. 'I'll have to take a sample and analyse it at the bunker.'

On the wall was a map, pinned in the corners. It showed the whole country, marked with red crosses – perhaps ninety or a hundred in all. There seemed to be no pattern to it at all. Some were in towns or on the edge of cities; others in the middle of nowhere. Imogen remembered what he'd shouted just before he tried to run her over.

You won't stop me . . .

'He's planning something,' she said. 'This map, whatever he's making – I think they're connected.'

Vetman bent over and picked up a black feather from the ground, turning it over in the dim light. As he did, a faint mewling sound made them all turn towards a dark corner.

'What was that?' asked Findlay.

Imogen darted towards the spot and found a stack of discarded crates and plastic containers and other rubbish. 'Bring a lamp!' she said.

Findlay carried one over and she began to lift the

trash carefully aside, looking for the source of the noise. And it wasn't long before she found it – a mound of tabby fur, barely moving. A pale eye caught hers, and it gave sad miaow.

'Rupert!' she cried.

The cat lay on his side, breathing shallowly. His tail was limp and he didn't move at all.

'Something's horribly wrong with him!' she said, reaching out and laying her hand on his side. She could feel the rapid weak patter of his heartbeat, and his stalled breathing. Her throat tightened. 'I think he's dying!'

'Stand back,' said Vetman. Imogen obeyed as Vetman lowered his face to that of the cat. After a few seconds, he breathed shakily. 'He's very sick indeed. I think he's been poisoned like the others. I need to get him back to the bunker at once.' He reached beneath Rupert's body and gently scooped him up. The cat flopped helplessly in his arms.

'Can we come too?' asked Imogen.

'There isn't time,' said Vetman, striding back towards the passage. 'You must go home, before you're missed by your mum and dad.'

'Our dad's dead,' said Findlay matter-of-factly, 'so he won't care.'

That seemed to catch Vetman off guard. 'Oh, I'm sorry, young man. I . . . I didn't know that.' He gathered himself. 'The fact remains, your poor mother will not understand why her children are out of their beds in the middle of a winter's night.'

Imogen wanted to argue, though she knew he was

right. The longer they were away, the more likely they'd be found out. But she wanted desperately to see that Rupert was all right.

Outside, the squirrel waited by the wizened tree. 'See them home, please,' said Vetman.

Then he pressed a button on his wrist. Big metal-feathered wings sprouted from his back, and his boots began to hum. He faced Imogen and Findlay. 'I'll do all I can for our feline friend,' he said. 'You have my word.'

Before either of them could speak, he left the ground with a *whoosh*, disappearing like a rocket into the sky, leaving a trail of smoke in his wake.

The Man With No Name

The girl was more resourceful than he'd expected. She'd tracked him down and nearly ruined everything. Never mind – it was just a hiccup, and he'd escaped with enough of the poison to carry on with the plan. And it looked as though the latest mixture was perfect; a single drop had been enough to finish off the wretched mog. He was only sorry he hadn't seen him take his last breath.

The Man With No Name hadn't slept at all since the escape from his den, and he guessed it was almost dawn outside. There'd be time for rest soon, when it was all over. Then he would sleep for days, sung into slumber by the howls of crying children. His lips curled into a grin at the thought of it.

The den had been perfect for creating his poison, but the launch site he'd driven to was something else entirely. Across the wall, a bank of monitors gleamed like the multifaceted black eyes of an insect – there must have been a hundred or so monitors that would show his scheme unfolding like a glorious tapestry of misery. And they'd never find him here, however hard they looked. It was just the spot from which to deliver death. He cackled, and the sound from his throat was like broken glass.

The Man With No Name carried the tank of poison to where his beautiful crows stood ready, their destinations programmed in, flight patterns set. A flock of death and destruction.

'Open wide!' he said, pressing a flashing yellow light on the screen of the control pad.

Each bird opened its beak in perfect unison. He took a pipette and squirted the poison into their mouths, where it would sit in specially designed receptacles in their bellies, ready to be delivered when it was time. The very next night, to be exact. A week before Christmas – when his gifts of grief would be loaded to the brim and shipped across the land.

He hummed his wicked tune to himself . . .

'Oh what joy, oh what fun! I'm the man with a plan, I am the one! My feathered beauties are all lined up! My soldiers are ready to put a stop to *anyone* who gets in the way of fear and death this Christmas Day.'

He skipped from one bird to the next, a lightness in his step he hadn't felt for years.

'I hate you. I hate you. I hate you all. Your smiles and your laughter I'll turn to a bawl. Very soon, very soon – I can see it all now – your moment of doom will come anyhow. Hah, hah!'

But as he worked himself into a hateful frenzy, distributing his poison, a niggling thought wormed into his brain. That man, with the girl and boy – the one who lived in the forest. Who *was* he? Not their father, that was certain, for what father would let his children roam about at night and put themselves in danger? The Man With No Name feared nobody, but there was something about the stranger that left him troubled and anxious, not to mention that he was dressed like nothing he had ever seen.

With the majority of the crows loaded up, a few spares remained. And looking into their beady eyes, a new thought came to him – an idea that tickled his fancy – a little scheme to make his enemies regret their interference.

'Don't want to be left out, do you?' he said to the motionless creatures. 'Don't worry, my beauties – you'll do your bit too. *Nobody* can make us fall – and soon they'll get what's coming to them all. Hah, hah!'

He moved a glowing digital dial on the control pad with his big bumpy finger and their red eyes flickered into life. Six heads cocked to face him, their sharp beaks clacking.

Chapter 12

'Are you sure about this?' asked Imogen's mum.

Ciara smiled. 'Honestly, it's fine,' she said. 'Take all the time you need. I know it must be hard.'

Imogen's mum looked at Findlay sternly. 'You be good,' she said. 'Do everything Ciara tells you and don't get in the way.'

Findlay scowled. 'I'm not five,' he said.

'Thanks again,' said Mum, before leaving through the front door of Pet Haven. Ciara had agreed to let Findlay stay at the sanctuary too while Mum went to work. Someone had called in sick and they really needed her to cover at the restaurant where she worked.

She'd ordered a taxi to take them home at the end of the day, and given Imogen money to order pizzas, promising she'd be back by ten at the latest. She fixed Imogen with a glare. 'I wouldn't be doing this unless I absolutely had to. I'm trusting you to be a good big sister.'

'Yes, Mum,' said Imogen, rolling her eyes.

What did that mean anyway? What if being a good big sister meant she couldn't be good in other ways, like helping animals, or fighting evil? Was one sort of good better or more important than another?

Imogen was glad to have her brother at her side after the night before though. Once Vetman had jetted off into the sky, the owl had guided them back along the road and the squirrel had followed them right up to the back door of their house. Imogen had put their muddy clothes straight into the washing machine with the contents of the laundry basket, hoping their mum wouldn't notice, but she thought she could still smell the rotten stench of Mr Byrne's lair in her nostrils the next morning.

Findlay gave a huge yawn. Neither of them had got much sleep.

'Are you feeling better today?' said Ciara. 'You still look a bit pasty.'

'I'm fine, thanks,' said Imogen.

Ciara said they could start with the walks, but even Pirate's fluffy face couldn't completely take Imogen's mind off the events of Quiet Lane. Her brother took Tilly, a fox terrier, and she went outside with Pirate. As they walked around the field, Imogen's mind was on Rupert. She wondered how he was doing at the

bionic bunker. She wished she had a number for Vetman, though something told her he probably didn't have a phone.

'Who do you think he is, really?' asked Findlay, as if his mind was on the same thing. 'Some sort of secret agent?'

'Don't be silly,' said Imogen, chuckling.

'He can fly!' said Findlay.

'He's just an inventor,' she said. 'An inventor who loves animals.'

In the back of her mind, though, she was thinking of how she'd found him the day before, tucked into the cradle, his chest aglow. Maybe that was an invention too, but it wasn't like anything she'd seen on TV or in a book. It had seemed . . . Well, almost alien. Like something from another planet.

The day wore on slowly, the children so tired that they felt as if they were wading through treacle. A few people came in to look at the animals, but each time the front bell chimed, Imogen's stomach tightened. What if it was Mr Byrne, coming in to try to adopt another animal? Or worse, he might have recognised her at his den and be hunting her down. She wasn't sure what she'd do if that happened. Scream, maybe, or get Ciara to phone the police. What could she tell them that wouldn't sound completely mad? He should be in jail for animal cruelty at the very least. But something told her that whatever he was planning was a hundred times worse than that.

At four o'clock, as it was starting to get dark, Ciara said they should go home because she was going to close up for the day and do some last-minute Christmas shopping. Findlay was playing on his game console in the corner of reception, and Imogen was finishing the feeding. There were just the cats to do. She went to the storeroom and took one of the big cans from a box that read *Premium Pet Supplies, for all your pets' needs, across the UK.*

As she prised open the lid she paused, a cold sensation creeping over her skin. She turned the can over in her hand. Under the list of ingredients was an address for the factory. She didn't recognise the name of the place, but in her mind the spark of an idea took hold.

What if the crosses on that map . . .? No, it was too horrible.

But now the thought was in her brain, it blossomed like a diseased weed.

She fed the cats quickly, barely able to focus, then grabbed her brother's console from his hand in reception.

'Hey!' he complained. 'I was on level six!'

'I think I know what he's up to,' she whispered.

'Who?'

'Mr Byrne,' she exclaimed. 'He's going to poison pet food! All across the country!'

Findlay frowned. 'How do you know that?'

'I think the crosses are pet food factories,' she said.

'Huh?' said Findlay.

'On the map! Think about it: every day they ship out their products. Biscuits, wet food, dry food, treats. If you wanted to poison dogs and cats, what better place than the sources of all their food?'

'I guess he *could* be,' said Findlay, 'but it's a bit far-fetched, don't you think?' He wasn't convinced.

But the more Imogen dwelled on it, the more certain she became. She imagined the trucks and vans leaving the factories, driving to supermarkets and pet food stores and vet practices everywhere.

'He has been testing it on cats,' she said. 'He wanted to make sure it worked!'

Findlay folded his arms. 'Maybe, but there's no way he could get poison into *all* the food. Someone would spot him, surely.'

Imogen had to admit that her brother had a point. It was a crazy plan. Almost seemed impossible. But the last few days had been completely crazy too. If you'd asked her a week ago about an elephant with an aluminium trunk or an alligator with a titanium tail, she'd have thought such wonders were impossible as well.

Ciara came in from outside. 'Your taxi's here,' she said. 'Thanks again for all your help. You've been terrific.'

Imogen said a quick goodbye, before she and Findlay rushed out of the door. They piled into the back of the cab and were home in no time.

As she unlocked their front door, Imogen glanced at her brother. He nodded, his mouth set in a determined line. She knew he was thinking the same as her – that they had somewhere else to be; somewhere far from their cosy sofa and tasty pizzas. Imogen left a quick message on their mum's voicemail to say they'd got home safely and then, feeling more than a little bit guilty, she and Findlay got their bikes and pedalled as fast as they could towards the woods.

Chapter 12

* * *

When they descended into the bionic bunker, Vetman was wearing a pair of goggles as, armed with a blowtorch, he soldered two pieces of metal together. He flicked off the flame and looked at them in surprise.

'Imogen! Findlay! What a pleasant surprise! I'm pleased to report our patient is doing well.' He turned and pointed to where Rupert was lounging on a cushion. 'It was a close call, but we pumped his stomach, put him on a drip and gave him some medicine. He needs plenty of rest, but he should be fine now.'

Imogen was delighted for Rupert and stroked him gently on the head. He purred gently and more contentedly than she had ever seen him at Pet Haven. 'We need to talk with you,' she said to Vetman. 'It's about the poison.'

'Oh, yes, nasty stuff!' he replied. 'We carried out some analysis. Very potent. Very toxic. He didn't have

181

much in his system, but it was enough to—'

'That's just it!' said Imogen. 'The poison is going to kill thousands of animals!'

Vetman blinked at the interruption, while the other animals across the bunker stopped what they were doing and faced Imogen. Whether they understood her words, or simply her tone, she didn't know, but they *were* listening. 'What do you mean?' Vetman asked.

'I think the map showed the locations of pet food factories,' said Imogen.

Vetman's face changed as he took in her words. His mouth twisted as though he'd eaten something rotten. 'He can't . . . That's too awful . . .'

'I wish we had the map,' said Imogen. 'Then we could be sure.'

'Oh, but we do,' said Vetman. He made a hooting sound and the owl swooped past, landing beside him on a bench. 'Let's check, shall we? If we could dim the lights, please.'

Chapter 12

The elephant reached out his trunk and used the end to delicately turn a dial on the wall. The lights went down. At the same time, the owl's eye made a clicking sound, and on the pale wall an image appeared. It showed a photograph of the abandoned farmhouse from the night before.

Findlay exclaimed with amazement, 'His eye is a camera too!'

'Next slide, please,' said Vetman.

The owl's eye clicked again, and another picture flashed up of the dead tree.

'Keep going,' said Vetman impatiently.

The owl flashed through the images, which showed the inside of Mr Byrne's lair, including the creepy animal skeletons and the scattered lab equipment. Eventually he settled on a picture of the map pinned to the wall. Vetman rushed across to a desk, opened up a battered laptop computer and began tapping the keyboard. 'Oh no . . . No, no, no . . .' His fingers moved quicker, his eyes darting between the projected photo of the map and the screen. Finally he looked up with a mixture of amazement and despair on his face. 'I do believe you're right, Imogen. Each cross does indeed match the location of a pet food manufacturer. Lights, please.'

The elephant tweaked the dial with his trunk and made the bunker bright again.

'I still don't understand how he's going to do it,' said Findlay. 'It's not like he can just walk in and pour poison into all the food.'

'No,' muttered Vetman. 'But we mustn't underestimate him.'

He glanced up as the tarantula dangled into the bunker from the room above, on a stretchy strand of webbing. She hovered beside Vetman's head, mechanical feet wriggling, and chittered in his ear. 'What's that?' he said. 'Birds? It's probably nothing to worry about.' From his cushion, Rupert gave a panicked screech and pushed himself up on to his paws. 'Now, now, you

have to take it easy!' said Vetman. 'You've been through an ordeal.'

'What's he saying?' asked Imogen.

Vetman waved a hand. 'It's probably just the medication,' he said. 'Our eight-legged friend said there are birds upstairs, and Rupert seems to find that alarming for some reason. I suggest everyone takes a deep breath and—'

The tinkle of smashing glass cut him off. It had come from above, near the top of the elevator shaft. The monkey gave a panicked hoot as a single black crow dropped through a small light portal at the highest point of the underground cavern. It was too high up at first for them to see properly, and it flew in lazy circles above them. Imogen screwed up her eyes. There was something not quite right about its movements. Not quite . . . natural. As it circled lower, she caught her breath. Its eyes shone a blood red colour.

'Something's wrong with it?' mumbled Findlay.

But Imogen was thinking of the crow she'd seen a few days previously at Pet Haven, watching from the roof. Its eyes had been exactly the same colour. Maybe it was the same crow.

A second crow arrived, then a third and a fourth. Two more followed. They made no sound and flocked in a perfect circle.

'Where are they from?' asked Findlay with a tremble in his voice. 'Are they friendly?'

One of the crows folded in its wings and dived towards Vetman. Only now did it open its beak in a grating caw. Vetman's eyes went wide and he ducked just in time as flames shot from the crow's mouth, scorching the air right where his head had been.

In a raucous chorus, the other birds swooped down, and Imogen saw that their beaks were filled with fire.

Chapter 13

Imogen ducked too, shielding Findlay with her body as the crows dived and released arcs of flame like miniature dragons. The air quickly filled with smoke as the fires took hold across the bunker. Soon benches and equipment and plants were ablaze. The budgies shrieked in panic, flapping through the dark clouds.

'Stop them!' cried Vetman.

The parrot shot overhead, chasing a crow with her metal claws outstretched, but her prey was too quick and veered away. Then the monkey leapt high, holding a tennis racket, trying to swing at another. The crow dodged, and blasted back fire that sent the monkey scurrying away. The alligator whipped his giant titanium tail hopelessly at the agile attackers. The crows swept mercilessly across the bunker, back and forth, until it seemed that everything was burning. Imogen rushed to grab Rupert just before his cushion went up in flames. Findlay was coughing as he crawled over the floor, his T-shirt pulled up over his mouth.

Then, as quickly as they'd launched the attack, the crows seemed to run out of fuel, and swept one after another through the hatch in the ceiling of the bunker, leaving chaos in their wake. As the last one followed, though, a cannonball shot through the air and crashed into it, sending the crow thumping into the wall, where it slid to the ground. Only it wasn't a cannonball, Imogen realised – it was the bristly ball of the hedgehog on his spring-loaded legs. He had scored a direct hit!

'Where are the fire extinguishers?' cried Imogen.

'The *what*?' called Vetman.

Imogen was losing hope, thinking they should

probably make a run for it, but suddenly there was a sizzling sound and she saw a dark lumbering shape moving through the smoke. The elephant! Water sprayed from his trunk, quenching one fire after another. She realised where the water was from, set down Rupert and grabbed a bucket from the ground, rushing to the alligator pool.

The alligator was using his tail to funnel water into buckets and tanks of all shapes and sizes carried by all the animals – even the spider came with small flasks. Imogen scooped up some swamp-water and rushed to the nearest fire, dousing it until it sizzled. The elephant continued to squirt water like a giant hose. The parrot and pigeon flew towards the blaze carrying a metal tank of water between them, and the tortoise came through the air on her rockets, sloshing water from pouches in her wheelbarrow. The kangaroo was bouncing on her spacehopper ball and the rabbit flew on her hoverboard, lugging pails big and small.

But it wasn't enough. The flames were all over the place. Many of the machines, various vials of medicine, cabinets of equipment and the beds of most of the animals were on fire.

Just as Imogen's hopes were fading, she felt a strange vibration through her feet; a rhythmic pounding coming from somewhere in the bunker. And then, through the smog, came a colossal shape, staggering low-down at first, but then standing up on two giant hairy legs, waving massive mechanical arms about and beating his

chest as he blinked at the sudden blinding light, and yawning so that his giant mouth opened in an unmissable growl.

A huge brown bear, over two metres tall, ambled into the bunker, brushing the straw of hibernation off

his dark fur with mighty bionic arms that looked like excavation diggers and he immediately joined in the fight against the flames. The guinea pigs and budgies threw surgical gowns on fires here and there. And with a big stomp of one of his giant pads, the bear quenched each flame in turn. If the heat hurt him, he didn't seem to care. Imogen and Findlay joined in, throwing damp blankets for him to stomp on.

Within five minutes, all but a few flames had been extinguished. Imogen could smell the smoke in her hair, and Findlay's face was smeared with soot, but thankfully neither were hurt. Everyone had played their part, but the bear had saved the day. He thumped his chest in triumph and roared, before dropping down on to all fours again.

Then, through the palls of smoke, Imogen heard choking and hurried to find Vetman crouching on the ground.

'The animals,' he gasped. 'Are they OK?'

Imogen waited beside him as the smoke slowly cleared, rising through the aperture in the ceiling. 'I think so,' she said. 'The bear saved us. Hey, take it steady.'

Vetman was trying to stand but he was still coughing, his body shaking.

'I just need to catch my breath,' he said. 'I'll be fine in a minute. I wish I'd had my suit on – it filters out stuff and helps me breathe.'

With Imogen holding his arm, he managed to climb to his feet on shaky legs. His face was a mask of dismay as he surveyed the devastation. She could only imagine how he felt at seeing the bunker in ruins.

'How was that possible?' she said. 'How can birds breathe fire?'

'Because they weren't birds,' said Findlay. He walked towards them with something dark in his hands. It was the crow struck from the air by the hurtling hedgehog, and it looked badly broken, one wing flapping uncontrolled back and forth. As he turned it over, Imogen saw a section of its feathers had been singed away. Her suspicions were confirmed. Beneath them, where there should have been flesh and muscle and bone, she saw metal cogs and gears and a frame made out of plates.

Vetman squinted. 'Well, isn't that interesting?'

It wasn't the word Imogen would have used. 'They almost burned this place to the ground! We could've been killed!'

'But we weren't,' said Vetman grimly. 'Let's see what we're dealing with, shall we?' Coughing again, he took the mechanical crow and carried it across to a workbench, where he laid it carefully on top. He called for tools, and the monkey leapt over, laying down a case. When Vetman opened it, Imogen saw it didn't contain medical equipment, but rather, shining tools – an assortment of tiny screwdrivers, callipers and a small drill. Vetman seemed to have forgotten about the fact the whole place had nearly gone up in flames as he donned a pair of goggles and went to work, prising open the fake bird to reveal the insides. She looked past his arm, mesmerised. Beneath the feathers, the crow was entirely robotic, with networks of wires and what looked like a large battery.

'Incredible,' muttered Vetman after a few minutes. 'Oh yes, look what we have here – a telemeter! Someone's controlling this machine with a transmitter of some kind, there's a battery and even a camera . . . all sorts. What a piece of engineering! Whoever made this has quite a talent.'

'It must be him!' said Imogen. 'Mr Byrne.'

'And if he sent them, that means he knows where you live!' added Findlay.

'My boy, that's the least of our worries,' said Vetman.

'Is it?' said Findlay.

As Vetman set down his tools and took off his goggles, Imogen understood the look of horror in his features.

'The poison . . .' she said. 'He's going to use the crows as drones . . . to deliver it, isn't he?'

'I fear you're right,' said Vetman. 'Exactly that, I think. With these crows, he can fly the poison directly to the manufacturing vats. A bird could slip inside a factory far more easily than a person – probably undetected. Even if it's spotted, no one would suspect a thing.'

'And we can't stop them,' said Imogen. 'We could barely stop this one. Those factories are spread out over hundreds of miles! There must be dozens of crows, and they might already be on their way.'

She felt like crying, or screaming, or both, when she thought about what could happen. No one working in the factories would know what was going on under their noses. None of the truck drivers would understand what they were delivering in their cargo. The pet shops and supermarkets and vets would sell the food, completely unsuspecting. And last of all, people would put the poisonous food into their pets' bowls for their beloved animals to eat. In a day or two, perhaps a week, dogs and cats in every corner of the country would sicken right before Christmas. The vets would be overwhelmed, and thousands of innocent animals would die.

Imogen looked at the bird drone on the table and its complex working parts. Though the plan was cruel beyond words, it was still remarkable that Mr Byrne, or whoever he was, could create such a realistic design. And it gave her an idea. 'If he's controlling the drones that look like crows, he must have a base somewhere. We could track him down and stop him!'

'Easier said than done,' muttered Vetman. 'He could be anywhere. If only we'd been able to follow one of those birds, perhaps we could've tracked him down.'

'Maybe we still can,' said Imogen. 'Can you fix this one?'

'I don't see why not,' said Vetman. 'It looks like a

wing hinge is broken; the frame is bent, and maybe the stabilisers are off a touch. But why would we do that? It's just a droid – not flesh and blood.'

'Because my bet is that it will fly back to Mr Byrne, or whatever he's called,' Imogen explained. 'It must have some sort of homing signal.'

Vetman clapped his hands in agreement. 'You might be on to something there!'

He took out his tools and leaned over the bird. For the next few minutes he worked in silence, as carefully as if the crow was one of his living patients. From time to time he'd mutter to the other animals, asking for suction, or an extra light, or a soldering tool. Where the feathers had been scorched, he replaced them with his own creations made of rubber and plastic, so that by the time he'd finished, the crow looked like it belonged with all the other inhabitants of his bunker, apart from its eyes, which remained dead and cold.

'How can we switch it on?' said Findlay.

'It just needs a jump-start,' said Vetman. He called to the monkey, who carried over a battery pack and wires. He attached the wires to the crow's feet. 'Get ready!' he said. 'If this doesn't work, it might go bang!'

'Hang on,' said Imogen. She pulled her hairband out and wrapped it several times around the bird's beak. 'In case it tries any more flame-throwing . . .'

Vetman smiled. 'Good thinking, young lady!' He switched on the battery. The crow jerked into life, its wings flapping as it sprang off the table, pulling loose of the wires. It flew in a circle, then darted straight for the wall at high speed.

'Uh-oh,' said Vetman.

But at the last second, the drone veered away in a loop-the-loop, before hovering in mid-air, head twerking left and right. Finally, having got its bearings, it shot towards the aperture in the roof.

'Follow it!' said Vetman.

The parrot went after the crow drone, the gleaming

crest of feathers on her head sticking straight up and her colourful wings spread wide, and followed it up and out of the bunker. Imogen listened until the sound of its snapping wings had vanished.

'Now what?' said Findlay.

'Now we wait,' said Vetman.

Chapter 14

Imogen's mind was full of doubts. What if the crow's circuits were too scrambled and it couldn't find its route back? Or Mr Byrne realised it was being followed and decided to make it self-destruct? There were so many things that could go wrong. And if they did, there would be no way they could prevent their enemy's awful plot from succeeding. Each time she went over any potential disaster scenario, she found it hard to breathe.

As they waited, Vetman's animal companions began the slow, laborious process of cleaning up the bunker. They pushed anything that was unsalvageable to one end. The squirrel used her tail to sweep up ash and smaller bits of debris, while the elephant hoisted larger pieces with his trunk. The big brown bear picked up some of the bigger clumps of debris too, with the alligator's titanium tail sweeping them into his excavator arms. The platypus scoured the floor with her belly and even the guinea pigs, the rabbits and the budgies scurried around, picking up bits here and there.

Imogen sat watching, with Rupert curled in her lap. 'What a day you've had,' she said, stroking the cat's cheeks with her thumb. 'What a day we've *all* had.' She checked her watch. It was almost six. They still had ages before Mum got home.

She watched Vetman as he pottered around the bunker. He was moving more stiffly than before, and every so often he would stop, his body racked by a horrible coughing. Perhaps he'd breathed in a lot of smoke, but she remembered the time in the woods when he'd keeled over when he was coming after them, and when she'd spied him in his strange cradle. She'd no idea how old he was, but he clearly wasn't well. Her grandad had a bad heart; maybe Vetman was the same.

One thing was for certain – he was a mystery.

And as she watched him, she recalled a detail from the night before, just before Mr Byrne's motorbike had roared out of the tree. They'd been standing over the gravestone – the one with the name Shep – and Vetman had said something. What was it? *Poor boy*, or something like that . . .

'You know who he is, don't you?' she asked. 'Mr Byrne.'

Vetman pursed his lips. 'I know that's not his name,' he said.

'So, you've met him before?'

'I knew the boy he was,' said Vetman. 'Not what he has become.'

'So, who *is* he?' she asked.

'A man who has nothing at all any more,' said Vetman. 'Not even a name.'

'Everyone has a name!' said Findlay.

'So, what's wrong with him?' asked Imogen, tired of the riddling answers. 'Why's he so angry?'

Vetman's eyes travelled around the bunker. 'I don't think it is just anger,' he said. 'Not really. I think something happened to him once, and it left a painful wound in his mind that has festered. Childhood trauma. Wounds like that are hard to heal. It takes a lot more than stitches, or antibiotics, or bionic implants.'

'That's what Ciara says about some of the dogs people bring in,' said Imogen. 'She says they're just scared because of their previous pain. She told me that's what *emotional trauma* is. They need patience and love.'

Vetman sighed. 'Ciara sounds like a wise person. I don't think our man with no name has had much of either.'

'So, who is he?' asked Findlay.

Chapter 14

Vetman rubbed his eyes as though he was very tired. 'When I told you I wasn't a normal vet – well – nowadays I'm not, but once a long time ago, when the bionic bunker was just a dream, that was indeed my job. People would bring their poorly companions to me and I would do my best to make them well again. I loved my vocation – getting to know them and their human soulmates. Making animals whole again, bringing happiness . . .' He trailed off. 'Sadly, it isn't always like that though. There are some cases that just can't be helped, or it isn't ethically right to help them, however much you want to.'

Imogen thought of the animals at the sanctuary who never found a home. The old ones with arthritis, or tumours, or those losing their senses or control of their bowels. Ciara looked after them as long as she could. Some of them died in their sleep, but with others there came a time when their suffering was too much. That's when the vet would come and help to ease their passing.

'Was it Shep?' she said.

Vetman nodded with a faraway look in his eyes. 'He was a handsome fellow. A loyal and loving friend. The boy brought him in with his mother. Something had happened. An accident. I can't quite recall, but Shep was badly injured. Too badly. A broken back, unable to walk. His spinal cord was severed. When the nerves in the spinal cord are badly damaged, it can be very difficult to get them working again, and when they were completely severed in Shep, there was really nothing I could do. Back then . . . it was a different time and place. I'm discovering new things all the time, with a little help from my friends, but that problem hasn't been solved even now . . . I remember all my failures and I carry their pain with me always. Vetman bowed his head.

Imogen wanted to hug him, and to tell him it was all right.

'Shep knew,' Vetman continued. 'I saw it in his sad

brown eyes. He understood his time was over. I told the boy's mum, but the boy wouldn't say goodbye. He told me I *had to* save his friend somehow. He begged and begged me to help, but I . . . I couldn't. It was impossible. And it wasn't ethical.' His eyes were moist with sorrow as he gazed into empty space. 'I did what I could.'

'You did what was right,' said Imogen.

'Yes . . . the right thing to do,' said Vetman sadly, 'I could have built him bionic wheels, but it just wasn't ethically the right thing to do for poor Shep in his particular situation.' He drifted away, lost in his own thoughts.

There was nothing more to say. No way to comfort him. And as Imogen watched Vetman reflecting on the past, her own mind turned to Pirate, at Pet Haven, without a family of his own. He was well now, but he was getting older. If she didn't adopt him, she doubted anyone else would either, and there'd come a day when he was too elderly or too frail to carry on. And when that day arrived, Ciara would phone the vet for him – to help him on his way. It almost broke Imogen's heart to think about it.

It wasn't long before the parrot flapped back into the bunker in a riot of colour, and landed at Vetman's side. Imogen held her breath as the bird clacked a message in his ear, her bright crest bobbing. She wondered how any human being could understand what a parrot was saying.

But Vetman clearly did, because he nodded gravely and thanked her.

'Did she find Mr Byrne?' Imogen asked.

'Not quite,' Vetman replied. 'She followed the crow as far as a large graveyard, but then lost sight.'

'The town cemetery?' said Imogen with a shudder.

'That's right – do you know it?'

Imogen nodded. 'You really think he might be *there*?'

'It seems a good hiding place,' Vetman replied. 'It will be out of the way; there are few visitors at this time of year. I don't suppose it's worth asking you to stay here?'

Imogen swallowed. A big part of her wanted to stay in the bunker, but she could see Findlay's eyes blazing in fierce determination.

'No way,' she said without hesitation.

'That's what I thought,' said Vetman. 'Wait here a moment.'

He disappeared into a chamber, down the passage

where she'd found him strapped to the cradle.

'Are you sure about this?' asked Findlay softly.

Imogen faced her brother. Her *little* brother. Normally it was she who had to be the brave one, telling him to be strong. Yet here he was, ready to go into battle at Vetman's side, and it was her fighting against the fear of the cemetery in her heart.

'I think so,' she said.

Vetman reappeared, wearing his armour again. Through his miraculous suit, which changed colour and shape like a chameleon, Imogen could see the azure glow around his heart that she had seen in the cocoon. It radiated like a pulsing beacon on his chest.

He raised his voice so it carried across the bunker. 'Listen up, my amazing bionic clan. You are my family. We have been together for a long time now. We have helped each other to heal and to get strong. I am proud of each and every one of you. Now I'm going to need all of you, big and small. We have a very important job to do together. You must leave behind the memories of when you were thrown aside, or felt useless. Today is your chance to show the world what you really *are* capable of, to show them why they should look after animals everywhere. Let's show all the people who threw you away that together we can save the day!'

The animals struck up a chorus of calls in response, filling the air with their din. Once Imogen would have questioned how they could understand Vetman's words, but that didn't seem important now. Whether it was the words themselves, or some deeper language spoken by humans and animals alike, there could be no doubt that they heard him loud and clear.

They started to ready each other. The platypus polished the alligator's spiky tail; the squirrel and spider fluffed up the feathers and wings of the owl, pigeon and parrot. The guinea pigs and budgies preened the fur of the big brown bear, still a bit crusty from hibernation and singed from the flames. The elephant hosed down the tortoise's wheelbarrow shell, while the bat dusted the soot off the hedgehog's quills, ready for action.

When everyone was ready, Vetman stepped on to the elevator platform and Imogen joined him with her brother. Then the elephant and tortoise lumbered up too, as did the alligator. The titanium-winged pigeon, the multicoloured crested parrot with her chromium beak and the bat with the X-ray eye popped up on the elephant's back. The hedgehog bounced on to the tortoise's wheelbarrow alongside the rabbit with the hoverboard feet, and the monkey carried the tarantula on his shoulder. The owl jumped up on one arm of the big brown bear, who picked up the platypus gently in his other mechanical arm, and the kangaroo tucked the guinea pigs and budgies in her pouch. Soon they were all crammed on the platform. Imogen looked at the chains with a little trepidation, hoping that they

could bear the weight of the entire bionic family. Then the squirrel jumped up on Vetman's shoulder, he pulled the lever, and up they went.

It felt like the strangest army ever assembled.

But together, as one family, Imogen thought they might just have a chance.

Chapter 15

The wrought-iron gates of the cemetery, topped with spikes, reared before them. Through the railings, the gravestones were bathed in moonlight. Rows and rows of the dead. Some new and sparkling, with fresh flowers laid before; others leaning and long forgotten, the words almost worn away and decorated only with weeds.

Imogen couldn't believe they'd made it from Vetman's cottage unseen, but the army had worked together without a sound to find a safe path. The birds had flown ahead, scouting the way, with the squirrel and the bat as lookouts on the flanks. They'd crossed roads and fields, avoiding cars and prying eyes, shielded by a thick mist blown from the elephant's trunk and wafted around by the giant titanium tail of the alligator. The brown bear and the kangaroo stuck close behind, carrying the smaller animals in his arms and her pouch. They all moved as one, a kind of animal mirage within a cloud of their own making. Vetman flew above them on the lookout, Imogen was crouched up on the elephant's neck, right behind his ears, while Findlay sat astride the shoulders of the giant brown bear, holding on to tufts of fur.

Vetman alighted in front of the gates with all of the larger animals. The birds had already flown over the gate and the smaller animals had squeezed through the bars.

'How do we get inside?' asked Findlay.

The bear lumbered forward and placed his mechanical excavator paws on the bars, ready to break them open.

'No!' said Vetman. 'We must be silent.' He surveyed the walls, perhaps three metres high. 'We can climb.'

And climb they did. Or bounce, or flap, or hop, or leap. One by one, the animals made their way to the other side.

The elephant helped to lift the bear and the alligator as they scrambled over, and then Findlay climbed up his trunk and on to his back. From there, he too scaled the wall.

'You next,' said Vetman to Imogen. 'Hold my arm and I'll fly you over.'

But now that the bars of the gates and the pebble-dashed walls of the cemetery rose up before her, deep-seated fear flooded Imogen's chest and squeezed her heart. It travelled down her legs and glued her feet to the spot.

'I can't do it,' she said.

Findlay, straddling the wall, called, 'Come on, it's not that high!'

He was right. The height was nothing – the wall was no further off the ground than their garden tree house. 'It's not that,' she said. 'You know it's not.' She turned to Vetman. 'This is the place where . . .' She didn't want to say it.

Chapter 15

'Your father?' said Vetman.

She took a step back. 'How did you know?'

'Grief isn't hard to spot,' he said. 'People wear it like a heavy coat.'

Imogen nodded. That's exactly what it felt like sometimes.

Vetman knelt in front of her. His green eyes gazed into hers.

'You're afraid, I know. I understand. I really do. I lost my mother when I was your age.' Then he paused for a moment, as if pained by the memory, before carrying on. 'But I need you, Imogen. Now more than ever. I thought I could do this on my own, but I'm not sure any more. I need you to be brave.'

Imogen thought of what waited on the other side – her dad's grave and the dash between the dates that was supposed to be his life. Her lips trembled. 'They just put him in the ground,' she said. 'Like he could have been anyone at all. They just wanted to forget about him.'

Vetman took her hand. 'But you haven't forgotten about him, have you?'

'No,' said Imogen.

'And he wasn't just anyone to you?'

She shook her head.

'Graves are nothing but holes in the ground with pieces of stone,' said Vetman. 'They're not important. They're only markers of our physical form. What's important is what's in *here*.' He gently folded her arm, until her hand rested over her heart. 'Memories, laughter, love. No one can take those away. Our physical form goes back to the oneness of the universe – but what's in there, deep inside all of us, lives for ever.'

Imogen felt like crying. She lifted her head to look away. She looked beyond him, past his head, and in the sky high above she saw the Dog Star twinkling brightly, just over the cemetery walls. Maybe it was just a coincidence . . .

'Like stardust,' she said.

Vetman's brow creased. 'Well . . . yes! Exactly. Stardust. Who told you that?'

'My dad,' said Imogen.

Vetman smiled. 'He must have been a really great man.'

'He was,' said Imogen. 'I wish you could have met him.'

'One day I will,' said Vetman. 'One day we'll all meet again in the stars.'

'He said that too!'

Vetman looked back over the wall of the cemetery. 'So how do you feel now? Do you think you can climb this wall?'

Imogen realised the weight from her shoulders was gone, the heavy coat was cast off – and at least for a moment she felt lighter.

'Easy!' she said. She rushed forward, leaping on to the elephant's trunk to hoist herself on to his back. From there, she took Findlay's hand as he helped her up beside him on top of the wall.

'I knew you could do it,' he said with a big grin.

The bear was waiting on the other side and helped them down, holding them gently between the excavator scoops of his paws. Last of all, Vetman floated up on the boosters of his boots. 'Can you stay here, please?' he said to the elephant. 'Do not let him past these gates if he tries to make a getaway!'

The elephant let out a very soft snuffle-trumpet in response.

As Vetman landed on the other side the animals gathered around. 'Spread out,' he said. 'Look for any sign and report back to me. He's in here, somewhere. I know it.'

The animals obeyed, flapping and jumping away in all directions.

Imogen stared around at the ice-crusted gravestones jutting from the ground as far as the eye could see, like a bed of frozen nails tearing at the belly of the sky. She and Findlay clung close to Vetman as they paced between the graves. Some were tiny – no more than plaques in the ground – while others had statues of angels or what looked like little buildings with crosses on top, marked with lots of names and writing. Some of the giant tombs were falling down, with gaps in the concrete where tendrils of branches and brambles were sprouting through, which to Imogen looked like clawing knuckles and fingers. It was unnerving, even with Vetman by their side.

From time to time, the budgies and other birds swooped back to deliver messages in Vetman's ears, but Imogen could tell the news wasn't good from the frequent sighs and comments like 'Keep looking', or 'Have you tried over there?' The cemetery was huge, having been there for more than three hundred years. There had to be several thousand graves, all spread out and surrounded by paths and flower beds. As they drew closer to the oldest, central part, there were no flowers, just weeds and briars. Imogen could faintly see tombstones from the eighteen hundreds. She shuddered as the clouds drifted ominously over the moon, like passing ghosts.

She was beginning to lose hope, when the little hedgehog bounced right up to her, then did a twirl, squeaking with excitement. Then he hopped away again.

'I think he's found something!' she said. 'This way!'

She followed the hedgehog, with Vetman and Findlay coming too. Her little guide stopped in an overgrown spot, and only when Imogen crouched beside him did she realise why her spiky friend had brought her there. Training her torch on the ground, the light shone over the unmistakeable tracks of a motorbike tyre.

'Found him!' said Findlay, peering over her shoulder.

'Not yet,' said Vetman. 'But we're close.'

Looking around, Imogen saw no sign of the motorbike, or the man whose name wasn't Mr Byrne. Nothing disturbed the chill evening air and the silence wrapped eerily around them. Vetman sent out a soft hooting noise across the graveyard. The owl flew over from wherever he had been searching, landing on a tall nearby gravestone and switching to his brightest beam. It was like a floodlight, illuminating the entire area and casting long shadows from the gravestones. The animals threaded between and over the graves, until the platypus called out with a strange buzzing sound. They rushed over, and found another track.

And so they worked, following the trail as it appeared and disappeared, until eventually they found themselves in a dark corner of the cemetery, among tilting tombstones speckled with lichen and with rusty overgrown railings tangled in brambles. Imogen brushed some undergrowth aside, looking for tyre tracks, and could see dates from the seventeen hundreds. As the motley crew approached the centre of the thicket, the cloud pulled back from the moon and the owl's light froze on the face of a truly monstrous, rectangular grey tomb – like a giant's coffin. There were flaking stone steps leading up to a great grey slab lying flat and covered in crusty moss and the tendrils of thorny bushes. Any writing had long since been worn away, but there were rubber tyre marks at the foot of the steps.

Vetman put a finger to his lips, but he needn't have taken the trouble. The animals were all quiet but for the flap of a wing or the shuffle of feet on the ground.

'We must find a way inside,' said Vetman.

The bat set off, flickering around the tomb, searching for cracks, but reported back that there were none.

Imogen surveyed the giant slab. It must have weighed a ton a least – impossible to move. If this was Mr Byrne's new lair, it was impregnable. The bear ambled slowly over. Perhaps he could lift it. The alligator shuffled silently alongside, trying to push his titanium tail beneath it. Maybe together they could shift the giant stone slab.

Chapter 15

Then movement caught Imogen's eye. One of the smaller gravestones to her right began to wobble a fraction.

'Look!' she said, her breath caught by what followed.

The ground began to tremble, just a little at first, but then more. One by one, more of the grave markers fell and cracked, toppling like dominoes. Then the slab in front of them seemed to shudder and rise like the lid of a boiling cauldron about to explode. Steam hissed from the gaps. It felt like an earthquake as the ground around the giant stone opened like a gaping chasm in the ground. The smaller tombstones fell inwards, like the rotten shards of teeth in a colossal mouth as it opened. Through the dust, Imogen saw huge hydraulic metal arms extend, lifting the slab higher and higher and prising the ground apart. From the deep, dark throat came a horrible metallic flapping sound through billowing smog. And then she saw it. A single red-eyed crow emerged from the smoky

darkness, flapping up and into the night sky, its laser-beam eyes darting.

'A drone!' said Findlay. 'We've got to—'

He never got to finish the thought, as from the gaping chasm streamed wave after wave of black-winged birds, emptying into the sky as if the mouth of death in the ground was coughing and spitting them out – filling the night with horrible flapping and shrieking cries.

Imogen watched them rise, and knew each one would be carrying the deadly poison of Mr Byrne's creation.

'Stop them!' roared Vetman. 'They mustn't escape.'

The monkey rushed across the ground and leapt with his super-charged bionic limbs, landing on a crow as it rose from the grave. The alligator used his tail like a giant fly swatter to bash the mechanical drones as they rose out of the chasm. The kangaroo caught another, hurling it down in a tangle of feathers. The bear left the slab and grabbed a fallen headstone, using it like a bat, knocking crow drones left and right as they escaped. The budgies swarmed a crow rising over the trees, pecking and clawing until it fell. The owl's beam switched back and forth like a searchlight, picking out the climbing shadows.

'There are too many,' Imogen muttered in despair.

But still the animal army fought on. The birds and the bat rose quickly and an aerial battle broke out above the graveyard as they swooped and charged the drones. The pigeon and the bat bashed them furiously with their wings, while the parrot pecked them with her chrome beak and brought them down with her steel claws. Sparks of collision filled the air like fireworks as they knocked the mechanical black birds one by one out of the sky. The crows cawed and swirled as they fell, silenced as they hit the ground. The birds and bat were soon joined by the tortoise, orange flames from the rocket handles of her wheelbarrow propelling

her back and forth, climbing and
diving straight at the drone crows,
butting them with her wheelbarrow shell and
barging them into the branches of the trees below.

The hedgehog bounced higher than ever before,
spinning and flailing his springs and spines at the drones
as they took flight from the tomb, and the spindly legs
of the tarantula telescoped out and grabbed at one or
two drones too as they rose, grappling them to the
ground. Even the guinea pigs joined in, crawling all
over the drones that had fallen and were attempting to
rise again, while the rabbit used her hoverboard like a
shovel, crushing their flailing metal wings and finishing
them off. The platypus held one down with her beak,
as the squirrel bashed at its frame with her tail.

But it wasn't enough. Despite the brave efforts of
the animal army, more and more crows escaped,
pouring out of the sinister mouth in the ground and
climbing into the night sky, rising over the graveyard.

For a moment, really high up, they circled, just as they had in the bunker. They watched the fate of their fellow soldiers falling to the bionic clan below.

Then suddenly, with a thump that shook the earth, the hydraulic struts folded and the gaping mouth in the ground snapped shut, sending out a wave of moss, dust and splinters as the giant slab closed the tomb solid again.

Imogen glanced at Vetman and saw his mouth open in horror. He clearly didn't know what to do either.

As they all looked on, the flock of doom circling above burst apart and with loud cawing noises each crow shot off into the night, heading in all directions. Imogen knew where they were going. She'd seen the crosses on the map.

They were delivering their deadly cargo, and there was nothing that Vetman and his bionic clan could do to stop them now.

Chapter 16

Vetman held his head. 'We failed!'

Around them, silence fell. The animals lowered their own heads, sharing Vetman's utter dismay. Imogen didn't know what to do or say.

But Findlay was looking at the sky still, deep in thought. 'Maybe not,' he said. Then he ran to the edge of the tomb and laid his hands against the stone. 'Help me push!' he shouted.

'What's the point?' said Imogen. 'The drones are launched. They're on their way.'

Findlay heaved with all his might, speaking through gritted teeth. 'But they're being radio-controlled by the Man With No Name! Don't you see? It's just like my truck. There's a telemeter inside – you said so – controlling speed and destination and everything, so there must be a transmitter. If we can find the controller, we can stop the signal – and if we can stop the signal, we can stop the drones!'

Hope sparked a green fire in Vetman's eyes. 'Gosh! You might be right. You just might be on to something!' He rushed to Findlay's side. 'Come on, everyone!'

Imogen joined them too, and marvelled as his sleeves rippled and pistons extended from within, as Vetman pummelled the giant slab with tremendous force. The bear also clamped his excavator arms on the slab and heaved. Every other animal joined in as much as they could. Every little helped. Imogen strained her sinews. All of them pushed and pulled together, groaning, but it was no good.

They fell back, panting hard.

'It's no use,' she said. 'We can't get in.'

Chapter 16

But then a snapping noise scattered all the animals and the alligator lumbered up.

'Out of the way,' said Vetman. 'He wants to try.'

Imogen backed off and watched as the reptile swung back his metal tail and with a mighty flick sent a slamming blow into the side of the giant slab at the front of the tomb. Spider cracks appeared across the stone.

'Again!' cried Vetman.

The alligator swung his tail once more, and this time the stone crumbled at the edges, revealing a small opening. Imogen heard fragments of rock tumbling inside into an empty space. Then a third monstrous blow caved in the side of the tomb completely, leaving a gaping hole of jagged stone, just wide enough for Imogen to climb in. Her fear had long since evaporated, spurred on by Findlay's enthusiasm. A faint light glimmered in the depths of the space within.

Almost at once there came a loud thunder, and Imogen jumped inside as the opening began to collapse in on itself. The bear swept forward, rising on his hind legs and placing his huge bionic paws under the slab to hold it up. He bellowed at Vetman, his muscles shaking under his thick fur, and Imogen saw they didn't have long. She beckoned Findlay between the bear's legs and into the passage on the other side.

Vetman tucked in his head and curled into a cannonball, with his suit changing instantly into what looked like an armour-plated armadillo. He rolled into the hole too, smashing rocks to either side, before unfurling himself beside her. And it was just in time. The quivering arms of the bear finally gave way and, with a mighty crash, what was left of the slab collapsed in a cloud of dust, flinging fragments of stone across Imogen's hair and face as she jammed her eyes tightly shut. With a crunching, shifting sound of settling rock, all was still.

When Imogen opened her eyes, they were in semi-darkness. Findlay's eyes were very white, peering out through the sooty dust that covered his face, and

Vetman stood up, shaking off the debris. There were just the three of them. The bionic clan was trapped outside.

Inside the tomb, a long passage led downwards under the ground towards the light. Vetman's chameleonic scales threw sparkling reflections across the massive hydraulic struts that had lifted the slab, before changing to match the grey blackness of his new surroundings. The air was dank with mould, and damp rivulets ran down the walls among clinging spiders' webs. It was just the kind of place where Mr Byrne or whatever he was called would be right at home. From further below came the sound of whirring machinery and cackling laughter. Vetman put his finger to his lips and they crept deeper into the deathly den of their nemesis.

As they tiptoed down, Imogen heard a scratchy voice singing a tuneless song.

'I hate you. I hate you. I hate you all. Soon I'll bring tears to all happy places and soon I'll wipe smiles off all happy faces. Ha-ha, tee-hee, my beauties have their systems locked on targets – and nothing can be done to prevent the carnage. You're way too late to steal my glory and tonight will absolutely end the story. Ha-ha, tee-hee, no one dares to stand in my path . . . and this Christmas you will all feel the pain of my wrath.'

The motorbike was leaning on its stand in the middle of the chamber. The Man With No Name stood with his back to them, in front of a giant bank of monitors. No more than a dozen were fizzing or blank, but the remainder showed aerial views of fields and farms, roads and towns – tiny sparkling lights far below. Imogen realised what she was looking at – the bird's-eye views of the crows in flight. Each one on its own journey to a pet food factory.

'If you've come to watch, take a seat,' said the Man With No Name, without even turning to look at them. He'd seen them on his security cameras as soon as they had entered.

'The best part is yet to come.'

'We've come to stop you,' said Imogen.

'Too late for that,' he said as he pointed up at one of the monitors, where a crow was descending. Tentatively moving closer towards him, she could smell the stench seeping from his clothes as she looked up at the monitors above her. There she saw a factory with smoking chimneys, and the crow soared down, over a chain-link fence, between two trucks and into a loading bay. It drifted towards a closed door. Just at the very last second, as it landed unnoticed, the door opened and a man in a worker's uniform walked out, munching on a sandwich.

'Hah! Right on time!' said the Man With No Name.

As the door swung closed again, the crow hopped through unseen. Now it was in a large warehouse filled with vats and pipes and tanks.

'Please – stop this,' said Vetman softly. 'You don't have to kill innocent animals.'

The Man With No Name spun round. His eyes were like gleaming currants deep-set in rising dough. Just as he turned to face them, Imogen caught a glimpse of what looked like a small computer tablet in his hand, no larger than a smartphone, its rim glowing red and its screen flashing with many small lights. He pushed it quickly into a pocket in his baggy jumper. Imogen shot a glance at Findlay. He must have seen it too.

'Innocent?' he said, spit flecking the ground at his feet.

'They've done nothing to you!' said Imogen.

The Man With No Name snorted. 'How could you say such a thing, child? You don't know me. You don't know anything at all about pain. How dare you! You know nothing of what they have done to me. How old are you? Nine? Ten?'

'I'm twelve,' said Imogen, hitching up her chin.

His eyes widened, and his lips parted to reveal great grey pock-marked teeth like square blocks of cement.

'Then let me tell you about the pain I feel,' he said. 'Each wagging tail is like a lash across my back. Each purr and happy bark is acid in my ears. Every child's laughter as they toss a toy, or dangle a ball of string, feels like broken glass beneath my feet. Any moment of joy between people and animals sends nails into my heart.'

His voice had risen to a crescendo, booming off the walls.

'Then I feel sorry for you, Mr Byrne,' said Findlay quietly.

The Man With No Name turned to Imogen's brother. 'My name is not Mr Byrne and I don't want your sympathy, you pathetic wretch. I want your tears, and those of every child in the land who ever loved an animal.'

'I think he's got the control transmitter in his pocket,' Imogen whispered to Vetman.

On the monitor beside them, the crow had reached the edge of a mixing vat. It hopped up and looked over the edge into the mulch below. Imogen held her breath as the crow dipped its head. Its beak opened, and . . .

Another shape zipped into view. It was a tortoise
– a tortoise with a wheelbarrow shell and rockets in
her handlebars. She must have followed it all the way!
She shot towards the crow and . . .

Whack!

The monitor blinked off.

'Yes!' said Findlay, punching the air.

The Man With No Name let out a long sigh and
shook his head. 'So what?' He waved an arm at the
other monitors. 'There are dozens more where that came
from. You might stop one, but you can't stop them—'

Vetman shot across the chamber of the den with his
booster jets, straight at the Man With No Name. He
ducked as Vetman scorched past, landing on the
opposite wall in a crouch. Instead of falling, he stayed
there, clinging like a gecko.

'Clever tricks!' roared the Man With No Name.
He picked up a table and hurled it with astonishing

force at Vetman. But Vetman was too quick, leaping clear as the table exploded into splinters and shards against the wall. Imogen looked up as Vetman scurried across the roof above her head, somehow defying gravity with the miraculous grip of his hands and feet.

'Come down and fight!' yelled the Man With No Name, 'so I can squash you like the pathetic lizard that you are!'

'I don't want to hurt you,' said Vetman. 'Can't we talk?'

A growl emerged from the Man With No Name's rasping throat and he marched towards Imogen. She tried to run, but he lashed out with his shovel-like hand and gripped her neck.

'You shouldn't have brought them here!' he shouted.

His skin was as rough as sandpaper on her throat as he lifted Imogen off her feet, so she was dangling helplessly.

Chapter 16

'Get off her!' cried Findlay. And suddenly he was there, landing on the back of the Man With No Name, hands clawing at the brute's black eyes, three-chinned face and cauliflower ears. The Man With No Name simply reached over his shoulder, seized her brother by the hair and tugged him free, then tossed him aside like a teddy he didn't want any more. Imogen saw her brother hit the ground in a heap. 'Findlay . . .' she croaked. She kicked and writhed, but couldn't get free.

Vetman scurried down the wall and approached with both his hands outstretched.

'Come closer and I'll wring her scrawny neck!' said the Man With No Name.

Imogen knew he meant it. She could hardly draw a breath. Her brother was dazed and hardly moving.

'Your quarrel is not with them!' said Vetman. 'They're children.'

'Exactly!' spat the Man With No Name. 'They're the very worst of all.'

The giant crusty hand on Imogen's throat tightened. Any more and she felt he'd crush her windpipe completely.

'I don't think that's true,' said Vetman, lowering his voice. 'Listen to me, *Trevor*. This . . . all of this . . . it isn't going to help.'

The pressure on Imogen's neck eased and air started to trickle into her lungs. She saw her brother stagger away. He was cradling his arm, as if it might be broken.

'How did you know my name?' said the man who didn't have one until a moment before. 'No one has called me that for years . . . not since my mother died.'

'My mother was the last person to use my true name too, Trevor. She's dead as well. So, I do understand. I remember when you came to see me,' said Vetman. 'When you came with your mother, carrying Shep in your arms, though he was bigger than you back then.'

'How do you . . . How can you . . .' His bulbous face creased in confusion, then it cleared like a passing storm and his eyes sharpened in fury. A growl escaped his teeth. 'It's you! It's *you*! You're the vet who took my Shep away from me!'

Vetman folded back his visor to show his face. 'Yes,' he said. 'It's me. I wish I could've saved him. I really do. But his spinal cord was severed, Trevor. He was suffering terribly. He was in pain. But, please, let Imogen go. She's a good person. She loves animals, as you did once.'

The features of the man whose name was Trevor squirmed with a mixture of disgust, anger and hesitancy, his eyes darting between Imogen and Vetman.

'Take off your armour,' he growled. 'Then we'll talk. *Man to man.*'

'Don't do it,' Imogen mumbled, but she wasn't sure if he heard, as the giant hand tightened around her neck again and choked her words.

Vetman licked his lips, staring desperately at Imogen. She pleaded with her gaze, but she knew he simply couldn't watch her suffer. He dropped from the ceiling and landed a few metres from them, just in front of Trevor's motorbike. Slowly he reached out and pressed a button hidden beneath his wrist. The helmet retracted from his head and the armour plating peeled off from his arms and legs. Last of all, the glowing azure breastplate of his suit fell away and beneath were his surgical scrubs. He looked smaller than before, like a shrunken man, with just a faint ebb of blue swirling like a cloud through his scrubs, throbbing with the beat of his heart. He now looked completely diminished, especially in front of the colossal man before him.

'There,' he said. 'It's just me now, Trevor. Just as I was back then. I'm terribly sorry about what happened to Shep. I really am. Your mother and I were doing our best for him.'

Trevor dropped Imogen like a stone and pounced on Vetman. He grabbed him by the chest, just around the faint orange letters V and M on his scrub-top, scrunching up the fabric in his fist. Vetman seemed to gasp for breath as Trevor looked deep into his eyes and Imogen could see unbridled anger growing like a volcano inside him. Then, with a single thrust, he hurled him across the chamber. Imogen flinched as Vetman's body slammed against the wall with a horrible thud and slid to the bottom like crumpled paper. She picked herself up and ran to him. Just as Trevor lifted his big metal-capped boot above Vetman's skull, she threw herself across his body.

'Move,' said the quivering giant.

'Never!' she cried.

As he reached down to seize her, she heard a voice cry out. 'Hey, Turnip Head! What does this do?'

He spun round. Imogen saw her brother was standing below the monitors. In Findlay's hand, raised over his head, was the control transmitter, its screen blinking with lights that she guessed were signals to the crow drones.

'Huh?' said Trevor, fumbling at his pocket. Then his head snapped back up, features set in a mask of pure rage. Imogen realised what had happened – when her brother had been flailing around on Trevor's back, he'd somehow pinched the device from his jumper pocket. Pride swelled to fill her chest.

'Do it!' she shouted.

'Don't you dare – I will rip you to shreds!' bellowed their enemy. He left Imogen and Vetman and began to stride towards her brother. 'Don't you—'

With all his strength, Findlay hurled the control transmitter to the ground. The device exploded in all directions, shattering into uncountable tiny pieces.

'No!' yelled Trevor. 'My beauties. No! No! No!' His cries echoed off the stone walls.

Across the monitors, the crows tipped forward. With no telemetry signal controlling them, they tumbled out of the sky. Trees and clouds and buildings shot past in an ever-faster blur, until one by one they hit the ground.

The monitors fizzled one by one too, and then all went dead.

Chapter 17

Trevor halted in his tracks. At first, he was completely still, his gaze fixed on the monitors. Imogen couldn't believe it. They'd done it! The flock was finished and the poison would never reach its many destinations.

But they were all still locked underground with their enemy, defenceless and at his mercy.

His great fists clenched and he began to tremble all over. His chest heaved up and down. He turned towards Imogen. His face, with its wobbling chins and scrunched-up nose, was just a rubbery mask now, completely still, eyes empty of all emotion. No anger, no hatred. Nothing.

Until a spark appeared, and his face came alive again. A broad and wicked smile broke out across his pale and bristled cheeks.

'You'll pay for that,' he said, his voice a hiss like water sousing ashes.

And then, just as Imogen feared he might attack them, he walked quickly across the chamber towards his motorbike. He swung a torn-trousered leg over the saddle.

'You think you understand pain?' he said. '*Real* pain? You will. Oh, you will. Killing you would be too kind a mercy right now. No. No. I have a different kind of death in mind. A death you can really feel. Oh, you will feel the pain. Hah! You'll see. You'll never get the better of me. The things you have done you'll come to regret. This will be a Christmas you'll never forget. Hah, hah!'

He kick-started the engine with a brutal thrust of his boot, and the bike coughed out plumes of black smoke. Vetman was still collapsed by the wall, holding his chest. He spluttered and grabbed the waning blue haze round his heart as if he was gasping his last. Imogen propped him up as best she could against the cold, dank wall.

Trevor pressed a button on the handlebars. Two shining metal cylinders slid out from the chassis, like machine-gun turrets. Imogen thought that they were all about to be sprayed with bullets, but instead the barrels sent out searing bursts of fire as he revved the engine hard. He drove the bike straight at her and Vetman.

Just as she thought they were done for, the bike veered away, bouncing across the chamber and up the ramp. The two barrels exploded with streams of lightning fire as the bike launched into the air and then hit the slab at the entrance with such force that the rock shattered to smithereens. The Man With No Name drove through the gap and out of the tomb. The noise of his engine slowly faded in the darkness beyond.

The animals all rushed in, led by the hedgehog bouncing high on his springs and the parrot, pigeon and bat in quick succession behind. All of the animals and the children crowded around Vetman.

'What did he mean?' asked Imogen's brother. 'We stopped him, didn't we? He can't poison the pet food now.'

'I'm so proud of you both,' said Vetman weakly. He tried to sit up, but sagged back, still coughing weakly and gripping his chest. His skin was white, and blood leaked from one ear.

'Don't move,' said Findlay. 'You're hurt.'

Imogen felt a tingle in her chest. The last words of their enemy haunted her, echoing in her mind. *This will be a Christmas you will never forget.* It might have been an empty threat, if it hadn't been for his horrible smile. The cunning, evil grin that told her he had another plan up his sleeve. A tide of terror crept over her as she realised exactly what he'd meant.

'Pet Haven,' she mumbled. Then louder: 'He's going to the sanctuary!'

'How do you know?' said Findlay.

Imogen shot a desperate glance at Vetman. 'He's seen me working there. One of his crows was on the roof! He's going to do something horrible!' She thought of the animals, locked in their pens, defenceless and alone, asleep in their baskets and beds. Ciara would be at home for the night. None of the other volunteers would be in until morning. And that's where Trevor was going, his heart brimming with hate and fired for revenge. She knew it for sure.

'I have to go!' she cried.

'Not on your own,' said Vetman. He took a deep breath, but grimaced in pain. He tried to stand again, only managing to get to one knee before pitching forward. The kangaroo caught him and cushioned his fall. He was in no fit state to go anywhere.

Imogen stared through the hole blown open in the

crypt. She frantically calculated the distance to Pet Haven in her head. On the motorbike, Trevor might be a good way there already. She tried to think clearly. Call the police? No, she had no phone. She couldn't see one anywhere in the chamber either, which was hardly surprising given what she knew of its nefarious occupant.

She began to walk up the ramp. She'd run if she had to, but Findlay caught her arm.

'You can't!' he said.

She pulled her hand free. 'He's going to kill the animals,' she said. 'I know it!' She looked past Findlay to Vetman. 'You know it too.'

Vetman shook his head, his face full of despair as he surveyed the chamber, every option in his mind hitting the same dead end as Imogen.

'I could send the bionic clan . . .'

'Too slow,' said Imogen. 'And what if they can't stop him?'

Chapter 17

She watched her words sink in. He wanted to argue, she could see that.

'They don't know the sanctuary at all,' she continued. 'But I do.'

He was shaking his head, mumbling to himself, as if to work out another option. But she already knew there wasn't one.

'You have to let me go, Vetman. It's the only way.'

He stared at her, eyes full of fear.

'What if things go horribly wrong? You could be in mortal danger.'

'I'll be OK. I have to try. I just *have* to . . . for Pirate! Please?'

Then his green gaze sharpened as it fell on his suit.

'Imogen, take my armour,' he said.

Imogen took a moment to understand. Was he really suggesting . . .

'No!' said Findlay. 'She can't go!'

'She can,' said Vetman fiercely. 'And she must. Take the suit, Imogen. It will protect you.'

Imogen walked across to the suit, bending down to pick it up. It changed colours even as she touched it. Amazingly, it weighed almost nothing. 'Will it fit?'

'She's just a girl!' said Findlay. His eyes brimmed with tears.

'She's much more than that,' said Vetman. 'She is whoever she wants to become.'

His gaze bored into hers, and in his green eyes a fire burned like the birth of distant galaxies. 'I believe in you, Imogen. From the moment I met you, I've seen the courage and goodness in your heart. Put on my armour.'

Imogen stepped into the suit and pulled it up her legs and over her shoulders, sliding her hands into the gauntlets. She hooked the helmet like a hood over her head. She felt very awkward at first, as if she was climbing into a giant onesie with a bucket on her head. But as soon as it was all in place she looked down and saw the scales ripple with a thousand colours, and a miraculous transformation instantaneously shrink-wrapped the entire suit to her head and body, so it fitted her like a second skin. She couldn't believe it – but then she had seen many things in these last few days that she couldn't believe. She looked at the complicated array of buttons on her forearm. 'But . . . I haven't got a clue how it works,' she said.

Vetman kicked off his rocket boots. 'You'll learn,' he said. 'Like you learned during the operation. Every little fear faced, remember?'

'Every little fear faced,' she repeated. Imogen took off her trainers and put her feet into the boots. They were way too big, but again within moments shrank to fit her feet like gloves.

'Squeeze your fist to climb,' said Vetman.

Imogen did as he said, and the boots sent a surge through her legs. She was propelled straight up, careering towards the ceiling. 'Argh!' she yelled, tipping forward and reaching out to stop herself colliding. But as soon as her fist uncurled, she plummeted again.

'Clench!' said Vetman.

She did, and just before she hit the ground she rose up once more, supported by the thrusters in her heels. For a few seconds she bobbed up and down, getting used to the adjustment. It was like rollerblading in the air really – you just needed to figure out the balance.

Findlay was grinning. 'That's awesome, Immy!'

There was no time to waste. She reached up and

pressed the button on the temple of the helmet, as she'd seen Vetman do. The visor slid down over her eyes and nose.

Vetman nodded, then coughed. Bright-red blood trickled from his lip. Imogen settled to the ground again. 'We need to get you to a hospital,' she said.

He shook his head, then made a clicking sound.

The bat swooped in from outside and landed on a workbench nearby. He spread his wings and his large bionic eye flickered and whirred. Imogen knew he was taking X-ray pictures of Vetman's bones, to see if anything was broken. The bat turned the extended screen of his wing towards him, so he could see.

As Vetman checked his own X-ray images, Imogen stared at them too, looking for any sign of injury. But what she saw didn't make sense. She knew what a skeleton should look like – they had a model at school – but Vetman wasn't like that at all. The bones were arranged all wrong – thin and arcing, a scaffold of slender branches. It didn't look human, and her first impression was of something else entirely. She suddenly realised what.

It reminded her of . . . a bird.

'Nothing broken,' said Vetman with a wave of his hand. And before Imogen could inspect further, the bat folded his wings with a squeak. 'I need to get back to the bunker. Findlay, will you help me?'

Imogen's brother nodded, his expression of responsibility making him look older. He actually looked a bit like their dad.

'Good luck, Imogen,' said Vetman. 'Do not be afraid. You can do this. I will always be by your side. Just talk to the helmet and I will hear.'

Imogen wanted to ask more about the X-ray picture, about what she saw – and about what Vetman truly *was* – but now was not the time. She'd known for a while now that he wasn't quite human – but he looked like a human on the surface. So how could he look like a bird under his skin? Part human and part animal? Then, as she helped Findlay to get Vetman on his feet, she felt the skin of his arms, really, for the first time. Remarkably, it didn't feel like skin at all – it felt like smooth silky feathers.

As she made to leave she hugged her brother tightly, and as he leaned his body into hers, she could feel the fast beat of his heart.

'Go get him!' he mumbled.

Imogen broke away, turned and ran up the ramp, to the jagged gaping hole in the stone slab at the entrance to the tomb. As soon as she was outside, perched on a pile of rubble, she squeezed her fist. Her stomach dropped into her rocket-boosted boots as she shot upwards, focusing hard to stay upright. Then, as the ground vanished and she climbed over the trees and graves, to her astonishment the inside of her visor lit up with a digital array and some kind of infrared vision. She could see clearly through the darkness. Metal-

Chapter 17

feathered wings sprouted from the back of the suit behind her automatically as an aerial map displayed on the visor in front of her. She knew immediately which direction to take. There was a small hissing noise, as oxygen streamed in from gills in the side of the helmet so that she could breathe easily, even this high up. Then another noise, like a whisper in her ear: she could hear Vetman's voice as if he were right next to her.

'You can do this. I am by your side.'

Chapter 18

Wind blasted her cheeks but under the suit her body was warm, even though the material felt thinner than the finest cotton. It didn't even feel like a fabric. Not that it mattered. Her only thought was to get to Pet Haven as soon as possible. In the distance she saw the village glinting, nestled in the landscape below. She squinted to get her bearings and, as if sensing her eye movements, the visor let out a tiny hum. The village zoomed into focus, growing larger.

'Whoa!' she said, feeling dizzy for a second.

She scanned the shape of the village and saw roughly where the sanctuary was. Then she angled her body and shot towards it like a comet. She passed over the patchwork of roads where occasional cars crawled like ants, and over illuminated buildings that looked like glowing lanterns. The scales of the armour had turned matt black, matching the sky around her, and Imogen knew that no one below would be able to see her soaring overhead. She was invisible as she whizzed past the town square and the twinkling Christmas tree, then followed the line of the High Street, tipping her body through the currents of air.

It took less than two minutes until Pet Haven came into view, and Imogen's heart lifted to see that all the lights were off. Perhaps she was wrong after all. Maybe Trevor's menacing words had just been to scare her.

Her hopes faded as some super-sensitive hearing device inside her visor picked up wild barking carrying through the air. The dogs only did that when there were visitors. She released the thrusters and slowed, descending gently towards the ground, until she silently touched down in the car park. Immediately she saw the motorbike under the trees to one side of the building, and as she crept past she could still feel the warmth of its engine. He hadn't been here long at all.

The front door of reception hung off its hinges, as if he'd simply kicked it open. Boot prints scuffed the linoleum floor within. The frenzied barking of the dogs grew louder. Imogen had no weapon, so she picked up the mop from its bucket behind the counter. What good it would do against a brute of Trevor's size, she didn't know. But it felt better to have at least something in her hands.

She walked through the vestibule, through the office and across the yard. The pens were on the other side, in a separate building.

Suddenly the barking went quiet, as though someone had pressed a button to mute them all at once. Imogen stopped, afraid of what she'd find if she opened the door. But then there came a frenzied yelping – the panicked sound of a single dog in distress. And although she'd never heard Pirate make that noise before, she instantly knew it was him and she could hardly breathe.

Casting her fear aside, she rushed into the kennels, skidding around a corner. The dogs, who normally would have wagged and barked and hurled themselves at the pen doors, stayed back. Some cowered in corners, while others curled up, trying to make themselves small. One or two were whimpering and shaking as Imogen made her way down the passage between them. She could see already that the door to Pirate's kennel was open, and quickened her step. A wail built in her throat at the thought she might find it empty, her dearest friend snatched away.

But he wasn't gone. Trevor was sitting in the pen, right on Pirate's basket. He clutched Pirate to his chest with one arm, the tattered sleeves of his horrible overcoat crushed around him. Pirate's eyes were wide with fear, showing the whites. When he saw Imogen he writhed, paws scrabbling to escape. But Trevor only held him more firmly, his knobbly knuckles white as his fingers sank into the poor dog's skin and fur. Even so, Pirate's tail still wagged when he saw Imogen. In his other hand Trevor held a syringe, the needle tip hovering above Pirate's neck. His black eyes swelled as he glared at Imogen in the suit and he chuckled.

'Hah. He's got an apprentice, I see.'

'It's OK, boy,' said Imogen as softly as she could. 'I'm here now.'

'So you are,' said Trevor. 'I've been waiting for you. You're just in time to watch.' He twiddled the syringe, his thumb on the end. 'You know what's in here, don't you?'

'Don't hurt him, please,' said Imogen. 'I'm begging you.'

She wondered, if she used the mop could she knock the syringe away? No. It was too risky.

'You can beg all you want,' said Trevor. 'Cry too, if you fancy. In fact, do cry – go ahead and cry. I want to see your tears. You knew nothing of my pain, but you will now!'

'*Why?*' said Imogen. 'Because you lost Shep?'

'Don't you say his name!' snarled Trevor. 'I didn't *lose* him! I didn't forget where he was, or leave him somewhere. He was *taken* from me by a man you know, holding a syringe a lot like this.'

Imogen could see his hand shaking. She dared not step closer. It would take him half a second to slide the needle in.

'I looked for him,' he continued. 'For the man who killed my Shep. But he had gone, or so I believed. To think he was here all along, under my nose.'

'He told us all about it,' she said. 'He tried to help. He really did.'

Trevor gnashed his teeth, his eyes fixed not on Imogen or Pirate, but on a distant spot in the past. 'He didn't try hard enough,' he said. 'He made a choice, and that choice was death. I moved away for many years, but everywhere I went it was the same. Children walking their dogs, throwing sticks for them, tickling their bellies, ruffling their ears, kissing their wet noses. Taunting me every single time I stepped out of the door. I hate their laughter and their disgusting happiness. I wanted to take all their happiness away, but that delusional idiot you call Vetman got in the way. He's not a vet – he's not even a man! He experiments on animals – and kills them when it doesn't suit his big ego!' Trevor paused for breath mid-outburst, before carrying on. 'And you helped him, so now I will take *your* joy.' He was smiling again, his lips a bitter curl.

'By killing the animals?' said Imogen. She put the mop aside.

Trevor looked down at Pirate. His gaze was almost tender. 'It's the only way to make the pain go away,' he said.

'It won't,' said Imogen gently. 'Not like this. Nothing that comes from hate will ever make pain go away.'

'Is that so?' snorted Trevor. 'And what makes you the expert?'

'My dad once told me that the hardest battle is with the enemy of fear inside yourself. I suppose that's the sadness and pain that we can't put a name on. Is that why you don't want a name?'

Trevor just grunted.

Imogen thought of the long days after her dad's funeral, when people came to visit her house, all saying the same pointless things. She thought of Findlay crying himself to sleep, and of Mum wandering through the house like a ghost. She'd wanted to fold them all up in her arms and make everything OK, but somehow she couldn't. Something stopped her, as if she was stuck in a bubble, floating in her own sad world, and nothing could burst it. It was only when she'd met Pirate that some of the pain started to seep away and she could breathe again.

Chapter 18

'You have to share your pain,' she said. 'You have to let love in. It's the only way to stop the hurt. When my dad knew he was going to die, we were camping under the stars one night and he told me that you have to allow yourself to be vulnerable for a while so that you can be strong again . . . I do understand . . . I haven't managed it either.'

Trevor's grip seemed to loosen a little, but he shook his head. 'You know nothing, girl.'

'Pain changes, if you let it,' said Imogen. 'It turns into other things. Some are bad, like fear.'

He glared at her. 'I fear nothing.'

'Anger then,' said Imogen. 'You're angry.'

'What of it?' said Trevor.

'Then it can change again,' said Imogen. 'Don't you see? I lost someone too. I thought they'd been taken from me. I blamed the world. I blamed myself. I blamed the people who didn't understand . . . who *couldn't* understand what he meant to me. It seemed to me that they had forgotten about my dad when he was put in a hole in the ground, and on his gravestone they reduced his whole life to a stupid dash. I was angry and afraid because of the pain. Sometimes I still am. And that dog you're holding – that precious innocent animal – he taught me that my pain could change. It could become love again.'

Trevor looked at her, then down at Pirate. 'A dog taught you that?'

She nodded fiercely. 'Pain is love, and love is pain – that's just how it is. They're two sides of the same coin. You loved Shep, didn't you?'

Trevor's bloated, whiskery face trembled and his head bowed. 'I told you,' he said. 'Don't talk about him!'

'Your love turned to pain, and your pain turned to hate, but it can turn back to love again.'

He looked at her and his eyes seemed wet. 'It's too late for that,' he said, shaking his head. 'It's too late for a monster like me.'

'It's never too late. It really isn't. Vetman isn't horrible. He isn't wicked – he's doing his best. And he taught me that doing the right thing is the best medicine. One love and one medicine – for all humans and all animals.'

'That's stupid. Just stupid,' said Trevor. 'This is the only medicine now!'

He raised his arm and was about to plunge the needle into Pirate's neck.

Imogen lunged forward instinctively. As she did so the tips of her gauntlets instantly morphed into claws like a cat's, triggered by the sudden movement. Arms outstretched, she scratched at Trevor's face. He let out a loud guttural wail that echoed around the kennel block, and Pirate yelped too. Was she too late?

The next few seconds were a frantic blur for Imogen as she kicked and grabbed wildly at Trevor's flailing tattered coat, trying to get the syringe. Then, in the madness, she saw Pirate's jaws clamp hard around Trevor's wrist, before kicking free.

Imogen sprang backwards as Pirate jumped clear. The suit seemed to have a mind of its own, or at least to sense what was needed, as she rolled backwards out of the kennel, grabbing Pirate as her gauntlets changed to soft-furred mittens. She slapped the bolt over on the kennel door, as Trevor roared within. She expected him to launch himself at the door, but instead he finally steadied himself and stood upright, his cries fading as he looked down at his leg. The syringe was sticking from his thigh, the needle plunged deep through his ragged trousers. He gawped, face creasing as though he couldn't understand what had happened. After a second or two he reached down slowly, seized the syringe and yanked it free, holding it in front of his face, his black eyes now bloodshot with pain and fear. It was half empty.

His eyes stared straight at Imogen through the bars of the gate.

'Oh,' he said quietly.

Then, like a wizened old tree uprooted in a forest, he toppled, landing with his face smushed up against the kennel door. Pirate let out a whine, sniffing through the bars at the massive prone body. Imogen grabbed for the latch and the gate fell open. Trevor's head rolled limp on to the floor, his chins squashed up against his cauliflower ears.

Instinctively Imogen reached forward and pulled his head up into her lap. He didn't seem to be breathing. His hulking body just lay there, motionless.

'Trevor?' she said, her voice rising in panic. 'Can you hear me? Trevor?'

His features didn't stir at all.

As Imogen held the giant heavy head in her hands she didn't know what to do. A million tortured thoughts rushed through her brain. Was this all her fault? Had *she* put Pirate at risk? And now had she killed the man whose name she'd only learned an hour before? He'd only come to Pet Haven because of her.

Then a breath trickled from his lips – a thin and rattling sound of air escaping from straining lungs.

He wasn't dead. But he was unconscious, and he was huge. She could barely lift his head, let alone his body. Pirate looked up at her with absolute faith in his eyes, but she still didn't know what to do. She couldn't just leave him. Before this had all happened, she'd even thought she might be getting through to him.

The other dogs were barking again. Maybe she could call 999 from reception. They'd send an ambulance. But what if they couldn't work out a remedy for the poison?

Of course, there was another place she could go. To someone who knew all about poisons and who might have an antidote. But how could she get Trevor to the bionic bunker? He was *ginormous*. And even if she did reach Vetman, the last time she saw him he was in no fit state to help anyone, even perhaps himself.

She reached for a fluffy teddy bear that Pirate had

in his kennel, and she put it under the massive turnip head as she backed away and paced up and down, thinking. She remembered Vetman's arm pistons that could punch through rock. They were strong, but how did they work? She tried to *will* them into existence like the claws and the mittens that had miraculously appeared, but nothing happened. Maybe the suit responded to movement, she thought, so she lunged forward with her hands out as if to lift the giant whale of a man who lay at her feet.

Nothing.

She pressed a button on her wrist. Tiny hair-like spikes bristled across her palms – they must have been how Vetman gripped the walls under the tomb. But it wasn't what she needed now! She pressed again and the spikes vanished. She tried another button. The suit seemed to fill with air, swelling from the inside until it was like a giant ball, cushioning her body. Imogen groaned. It was cool, but it didn't help. She had no idea how to control the suit. She muttered to herself, 'If only he was here.'

Then a whisper came from inside the helmet. 'But I am here. I told you, I am by your side.'

'Vetman?' she asked.

'Yes, Imogen. Well, it looks like you've been busy, now, haven't you?'

'Ummm, yes. But he's injected *himself* with the poison. I can't even move him!'

Without warning, the suit began to transform into something mechanical around her. The pistons emerged from the sleeves, struts popped out of the sides of the legs, and four more arms snaked out of the back of the suit and dangled in front of her like the tentacles of an octopus.

'Wow!' she said.

'What are you waiting for?' came Vetman's voice.

The octopus tentacles slithered under and around Trevor and hoisted him up from the ground. It was amazing – he felt almost as light as the teddy bear under his head. With Pirate at her heels, she began to drag him down the corridor, still not convinced she could actually lift him, and even less confident that she could fly with him. After all, she was just a girl, and he was a giant of a man.

'But you're not *just* anything, Imogen,' said Vetman, as though he'd read her mind. 'You are whoever you want to become.'

Pirate looked up at her.

'I can't take you too,' she said. 'I'm sorry!'

Pirate cocked his head and seemed to understand. He turned and wandered back towards his kennel.

'I'll see you very soon,' said Imogen. 'I promise.'

She pulled Trevor out into the yard.

Imogen had no idea if the boot thrusters would be strong enough to lift them both, but she needn't have worried. With her multiple arms cradling him, she squeezed her fist and the jets fired up. Slowly, wobbling more than a little, they both rose into the air. Small funnels rose out of the tentacles like the suckers of an octopus and seemed to suck at the air like tiny vacuum cleaners before blasting it out behind her and propelling her across the sky.

Imogen couldn't believe it. The suit seemed to

levitate, defying gravity as it moved effortlessly through the sky. She knew enough of the world to realise then that her suspicions about Vetman were true. His suit of armour was not of this planet – no human technology came close to the capabilities of the suit she wore. It had all the special adaptations of animals on Earth, but it seemed to bend the laws of physics. It didn't weigh anything itself yet could carry huge weight. And if Vetman's inventions were from somewhere beyond this world . . . Trevor had clearly said Vetman wasn't even a man . . . What exactly was he? An alien?

As she set off towards the forest on the other side of the village, she dared not go too fast, in case the wind ripped her passenger from her grip, or too high. For what if the propulsion system in the suit failed? So she flew low over the treetops, skirting electricity wires and roofs. She couldn't worry now that someone would see her – a life was at stake. Even if it was the life of their enemy.

Chapter 19

It seemed to take a lot longer than her first trip, so when the woodland and Vetman's cottage came into view Imogen breathed a sigh of relief. It looked different from the air – nearer to the trees than she recalled. She flew down and landed with her massive cargo on the wooden step with a loud thump.

She didn't even know for sure if Vetman and his bionic clan had made it back from the cemetery yet. 'Help!' she called. 'Finn? Vetman?'

Thankfully, there was a loud thumping noise from inside the cottage and, from the doorway, the giant brown bear emerged, took one look and immediately scooped Trevor from Imogen's tentacles with his bionic excavator arms. Imogen's extra limbs disappeared back into nowhere just as quickly as they had arrived and she followed the bear down the hall, which this time seemed much shorter than before. She pulled the lever on the wall and they descended in the elevator to the bunker below. The animals were all waiting beneath. Vetman stumbled towards her as the bear laid down the huge man on a fire-scorched operating table. If he was breathing now, Imogen couldn't see it. Findlay hovered behind Vetman. His eyes lit up on seeing her, but when he saw the giant body of their enemy, his lips parted in astonishment.

'Why've you brought him *here*?' gasped her brother.

'There was an accident,' Imogen explained. 'I didn't know what else to do!'

Vetman didn't say anything, and Imogen thought that he still seemed weak, but his assistants were ready and sprang into action. With a single tug, the alligator ripped off Trevor's crumpled coat, and with a few quick shears of her chromium beak the parrot cut away his crusty jumper. Beneath it, his skin smelled like rotting fungus, making Imogen's eyes water. Holding her nose with one paw, the kangaroo handed over a stethoscope with the other and Vetman placed it on Trevor's chest.

'Very weak,' he muttered. 'And he hasn't been taking care of his body for a long time, which doesn't help. How much poison was there?'

'A lot, I think. Half a syringe – whatever that is,' said Imogen. 'Is there anything you can do?'

Vetman took off the stethoscope and placed it on the monkey's ears. 'Monitor him, please.' He ran a hand through his hair, thinking. 'If it was in his stomach, he might have a chance, but it's in his bloodstream now, in every part of his body already, destroying his organs, just as he had intended for all of the poor dogs and cats.' He looked around his bunker at the mess. 'Normally I'd suggest extra-corporeal blood filtration, but the equipment's wrecked . . . He really has ended up destroying himself.'

'What about a hospital?' said Findlay.

Vetman shook his head doubtfully.

Imogen had known it might come to this, of course, from the moment she saw the needle sticking out of his leg. But to think he might die, right here in the bunker . . . even after all he'd done. She couldn't bear it.

'I was talking to him,' she said. 'About Shep . . . about Dad. He's not all bad. Deep inside there's something good left. I know it.'

'This isn't your fault, Imogen,' said Vetman. 'None of this is your doing.'

The monkey hooted, and as Vetman listened to the stethoscope again, he sighed deeply. 'His heart's slowing right down. We're losing him.'

Findlay pressed himself against Imogen, and she

wanted to cover her brother's eyes. He was too young to see someone die.

Vetman hesitated for a moment, muttering to himself in what sounded like angry curses. Then his green eyes shone brighter than Imogen had ever seen them before. He gave one firm, decisive nod, then gripped the side of the operating table. He leaned close, until his face was level with his patient. 'Stay with me, Trevor,' he said. 'I don't know if this will work.'

He whistled loudly. The budgies brought him a mask, which the squirrel rapidly hooked around his ears. The guinea pigs dipped some gloves in iodine and he popped them on. The elephant hoisted up a bucket of water, which the tortoise boiled with a flame from one of her rockets. Then the pigeon and the parrot threw several surgical instruments into it to sterilise

them. The bear's excavator hands couldn't feel the heat, so he grabbed the bucket and popped it on to the wheelbarrow-back of the tortoise, who had crouched as a table beside Vetman. His fingers found a scalpel from the tray of tools. Imogen flinched, wondering what he was about to do. Behind them the other animals bustled around collecting vials, jars, tubes and whatever other contraptions they could gather that hadn't been ravaged by the fire.

Vetman held the scalpel over Trevor's chest and leaned in over him. But just as he was about to cut, he pulled back from the table.

'There is no time,' he said, almost to himself.

He stood back, as all of the animals stopped whatever they were doing and looked at him. Findlay's lips were parted in wonder. Imogen gazed at the scalpel dangling in Vetman's hand. Was he giving up?

But then he gave a brisk nod, as if he'd come to a sudden decision. He turned the blade towards himself, gripped his scrub-top and sliced through it in a vertical line – right through the V and M. He placed the scalpel down and tore open his top. Underneath, above his heart, she saw the strange blueish tattoo again. It was a very strange swirl of shining flesh – and yet, not flesh. Now, up close, it looked like neither human nor animal, but maybe a bit of both. Imogen had never in her life seen anything like it.

Vetman pulled off his surgical gloves and mask. Taking a deep breath, he reached out and placed his bare hand on Trevor's chest. He looked more like a corpse than ever – just meat on a slab.

Vetman closed his eyes.

'What's he doing?' asked Findlay.

The marks on Vetman's flesh began to . . . move. Imogen couldn't take her eyes off them. They rippled and coiled, like a galaxy of stars swirling beneath his skin, slow at first but then faster and faster. At the same time, they changed colour, as though dyes of different hues were flowing through his blood vessels. Turquoise, aquamarine, sapphire and then radiant azure. It made no sense at all, but the image of the other-worldly skeleton came to Imogen's mind again. She was more certain than ever: nothing about Vetman, despite his outward appearance, was human.

Beside her, Findlay stiffened and she felt his fear, but she put her arm around his shoulders to reassure him. As they both looked on, a rippling blue tide like a stream of light crept from Vetman's chest, along his shoulder blade and down his arm, past his elbow and into his hand. Sweat was beading across his brow, and his lips were pressed together so hard they became a pale, bloodless line. Whatever he was doing, it clearly hurt.

When the pigment reached his hand, it spread out from his fingertips, leaking like rivulets of ink on to Trevor's chest, where it sank into his skin like water into parched soil. Vetman's legs were trembling, as though he was forcing every last drop of whatever it was from himself and into the patient before him. The sweat was seeping through his tunic and he began to shake violently.

'Come on, Trevor,' he whispered. 'Take it, please. Take it . . . It's all I've got.'

Take what? thought Imogen. She had no idea what was happening.

Trevor's fingertips twitched, and around the table the animals began to flap and chatter. Then his chin jerked, his eyelids fluttering, as if he was having a bad dream.

'Don't turn your back on me, Trevor,' said Vetman. 'There are no conditions . . . Argh!'

He suddenly fell back as if he'd been punched and collapsed on to the ground. As Imogen rushed to help him, the man on the table gave a huge gasp, as if he was sucking in all the air in the room. He sat bolt upright. His chest heaved up and down as his head snapped this way and that. His eyes were open wide in shock as he took in the animals surrounding him, before he finally settled his gaze on Vetman, who lay on the ground, his breath no more than a shallow wheeze. On his chest, the blue mark had faded to pale pink. It looked withered like scar tissue, all colour gone.

'He saved your life,' Imogen said to Trevor.

'No . . . No . . . No . . .' he croaked, but his fingers grabbed at his own chest as though he could feel something there still.

'Yes!' said Findlay. 'He gave you something.'

'He gave you the coloured stuff from his heart,' said Imogen.

Trevor's face crumpled, shaking his head in disbelief.

'Now you need to choose love, Trevor, you really do – it will heal the pain.'

A howl of horror escaped his lips and he clambered

from the operating table, gathering his torn clothes over his pale flesh. He pushed the animals roughly aside and staggered towards the elevator. At first no one stopped him – their eyes were all fixed on Vetman, their saviour, in a heap beside the operating table.

Finally, the bear, elephant and alligator rushed to block his path. He seemed bewildered at first, trying desperately to cover his body, as if he was ashamed for anyone to see him so exposed and vulnerable.

But as soon as his old crusty coat was pulled around his shoulders again, it was as if a cloak of darkness enveloped him. He flew into a furious rage.

'Out of my way!' he spat.

They didn't move an inch.

Trevor's eyes darted around, as if searching for another escape route. Then he headed between two tables, on which rested several vials rescued by the animals from the charred medicine cabinet during the fire. He snatched them up, one at a time, tugging out the corks and sniffing at their insides. Imogen had no idea what he was looking for – more poison?

At last he seemed to find a couple he wanted – two large glass containers sloshing with clear liquid. And with the alligator closing in, he stomped back in their direction. Imogen moved to shield her brother, but Trevor only came so close before lifting his foot and bringing it down hard on Vetman's armoured suit, which lay on the floor. He smashed the helmet to smithereens.

'Hah, I hate you, I hate you all – and I will annihilate you. You should have let me die in my pain. For now, it is you that will feel the shame. An eye for an eye, a tooth for a tooth . . . soon you will all face the terrible truth. You took everything I ever cared about and you didn't care when I was crying, so now it's you that'll be dying. You're all gonna come an awful cropper and this time I'll finish you off good and proper. Hah, hah!'

He flicked on one of the big cooling fans near

Vetman's operating table. Then he reached into his deep pocket and pulled out a rubber gas mask. It looked like the sort of thing scientists used in labs when carrying out dangerous experiments. He pulled it over his head.

Then, with a last glare at Vetman, he hurled the flasks against the fan, shattering them. At once, a noxious smoky gas seeped into the air of the bionic bunker. The dense fog consumed all of the animals, the children and Vetman.

'What is it?' asked Findlay, his voice quaking.

'I don't know,' said Imogen, but as the bear wobbled, she guessed. 'Anaesthetic gas! Get down!'

She pressed Findlay to the floor as the bear crashed down on to his side. The elephant stumbled against a wall. The alligator reared up on his tail to escape, but fell over backwards and lay motionless. The budgies fell from the air as the gas enveloped them while others sought the upper reaches to stay out of the way.

'Serves you right, you stupid creatures,' said Trevor, his voice muffled behind the mask. 'I have nerves of steel and a heart of stone and my job's not done until it's done. I hope this gas knocks you all out dead . . . and one thing's for sure, the man with a plan will always be one step ahead! Hah, hah!'

With that, he leapt on to the elevator platform, pulled the lever and up to the surface he went, the shaft closing tightly beneath him.

Findlay was coughing and Imogen felt suddenly woozy as she crawled across the floor, past smaller animals who had already succumbed to the gas. The squirrel was sprawled out; the tortoise lay on her side. She wanted to help them but she barely had the strength to help herself. At last, weakened by the gas, her arms gave way and she collapsed too, like a puppet with its strings cut.

Chapter 20

Through the barely open cracks of her eyelids, Imogen saw a shape shooting through the air. At first, she didn't understand, but as she saw the springs quivering beneath him, she realised it was the hedgehog. With every leap, he rose through the fog of gas, higher and higher each time.

But what was he doing?

With one final, gravity-defying leap, he collided with a duct running across the ceiling, puncturing it with his spikes. A loud sucking noise ripped through the bunker, and almost at once the white cloud began to stream towards the opening. The air cleared and

Imogen could breathe freely once more. She could feel her limbs working again, and pulled herself towards her brother, who was waking too.

One by one the animals stirred, shaking their groggy heads.

But Vetman was gasping, struggling for breath and grasping his chest. Imogen shook her head, still unfocused.

'Vetman?' she said, as she crouched down where he lay. Only his eyes moved in his face, rocking to meet hers. The bright-green orbs had been replaced by deathly hollows in his pallid skull.

His lips formed a faint smile. 'It's over,' he said.

'Are you OK?'

'I need to . . . rest,' he said.

'Finn, help me get him up!' she said.

Findlay didn't hesitate and he gently lifted Vetman's arm over his shoulder. Immediately the monkey joined in and between them they hoisted him to his feet. But he was limp and practically lifeless, his head sagging forward on his slouched shoulders – just a wisp of the man he had been before.

'Are we taking him to hospital?' asked her brother.

'No,' she said, nodding towards the arch at the other side of the bunker. 'That way.'

Together, they staggered forward and immediately all the other animals came to help as well. The monkey took one leg, and the elephant gently lifted the other, as the bear scooped up Vetman's shoulders more gently than he had ever lifted anything. Imogen and Findlay held his arms. The alligator cleared a path through the debris, helped by the bobbing hedgehog, squirrel, rabbit and kangaroo. They made their way along the glowing corridor marked with hieroglyphs on the walls. The flocking birds and the bat flew overhead, and the guinea pigs scurried behind until they reached the laboratory alcove where Imogen had seen Vetman in his cocoon. The tarantula and the bat joined with the pigeon and parrot as they unfurled large iridescent leaves which formed a kind of shell around the cradle inside. Findlay was staring around, amazed.

'Put him in there!' panted Imogen.

'What is this place? What is that thing?' asked Findlay.

'I think it's some kind of rejuvenation pod,' said Imogen. 'I found him here before. Well, actually, I have no idea what it is, but it seemed to help him and whatever was going on with his heart the last time he was weak.'

Now Imogen noticed for the first time that the cocoon was inside a ring of what looked like Celtic symbols on the floor beneath, out of which came the multicoloured cable she had seen before, straight up and into the cradle.

The animals gently carried Vetman like a baby, until

his body was safely nestled inside the high-tech petals. As Imogen touched them, though they looked like what she had seen covering a spacecraft in a movie once, they felt as soft and warm as silk left drying in the sun. The cocoon was like Vetman's skin – it looked quite different than it felt. The strange petals curled around Vetman's motionless form like an embrace. In their midst, he breathed a long sigh. It was as if the past and the future came together inside the incredible cradle of healing.

'What now?' asked Findlay. 'Will he be OK?'

Imogen wished she knew. 'Is it your heart?' she said to Vetman.

Vetman's eyes blinked slowly. 'That's close enough,' he whispered softly, grimacing. 'You must go now. Before you're missed.'

'No,' said Imogen. 'We're staying here. We're not leaving you alone.'

Vetman frowned. 'But I'm not alone, Imogen. Look

around. I'm never alone among my clan. They're my family. They are by my side. They will look after me.'

'But you're sick!' she said. 'Don't try to lie. I saw what happened. He took it from you – whatever that blue stuff is.'

'He took nothing,' said Vetman. 'It was mine to give, with no expectation of return – unconditional.' He shifted his body, pain clouding behind his green eyes.

'But what was it?' she asked. 'Some sort of energy? Life force?'

'Those are words for it. There are others . . . It's the one medicine that heals everything.'

'What's that supposed to *mean*?' said Imogen. 'Why do you talk in riddles?'

'Because you know what it is,' he said. 'It's everywhere and everything. The dust of stars, in its purest, most perfect form. Eternal and indestructible.' His eyes glowed weakly and he reached out both hands. Findlay took one, and she the other. And in his touch, she understood.

'It's *love*,' she said. 'That's it, isn't it? Unconditional love.'

'Isn't everything?' he said. 'If you let it be so. Now, off you go.'

'Will we see you again?' she asked.

'Of course,' said Vetman, smiling. 'Just look. I will never be far away.'

'But will you be OK? Will this pulsing cable thing be enough?' she asked.

'Everything passes, Imogen, everything passes . . . One day maybe we can go to the island together . . . where it all began.'

Vetman was now drifting in and out of sleep and becoming incoherent.

'What island? Where? Is this cocoon thing the island?' Imogen asked.

He didn't answer. Though his eyes were open a

fraction, it seemed that he had drifted into oblivion.

Imogen gently placed his hand back on a glowing orange petal, and Findlay did the same on the other side of the cocoon. The shining cradle folded its petals gently around him. Like Vetman, it was surely not of this world.

Beneath him the cable pulsed like a stem feeding a flower, and a blue-tinged aura slowly ebbed along it towards Vetman's heart inside the cradle.

Imogen looked around at all the animals with tears welling up in her eyes. All of *their* eyes were on Vetman, as if the very essence of their love was wrapped like a warm blanket around him too.

She gave a little respectful nod and leaned over one last time to check that Vetman was still breathing. He was – softly, peacefully, his heart beating in harmony with the pulses.

Just as she was about to let go, he softly squeezed her hand. His lips were moving soundlessly, and she leaned right in, as far as she could. She wasn't sure if she could actually hear his voice, or just feel it on her cheek. It seemed to come from somewhere far away.

'One last thing, Imogen . . . Remember . . . the thing you are searching for is always inside you . . . It always was . . . and always will be . . . and I am by your side.'

The grip loosened on Imogen's hand and he opened his emerald eyes briefly one last time, looking at her with his deep kindness. Then his eyes closed and it seemed he had drifted to his own distant world.

'Time to go,' she mumbled.

She and her brother turned reluctantly towards the passage that would lead back towards the bionic bunker and the platform. And to *their* own world, which would be forever changed.

Epilogue

When Imogen looked out of the window a few days later, the world was indeed transformed. A thick blanket of snow covered the back garden, making marshmallow lumps out of the shrubs and bushes. The branches of the chestnut glistened with sugary snow. The Wilderness beyond the fence wasn't in the least scary now, but rather a winter wonderland, the pine trees jutting up from the blanket of whiteness like candles on a giant Christmas cake.

'A white Christmas!' she said.

Her brother stirred, rubbing his eyes, but they practically popped out of his head when he saw the snow outside. He thrust off his duvet and rushed to the window. 'Let's build a snowman!' he said. 'No, a snow bear!'

'Or a snow elephant!'

'Or a snow tortoise!'

Imogen grinned as they threw on their dressing gowns. Mum's door was open, and there were noises of rustling from downstairs. They rushed down and found her with a mug of tea in the kitchen.

'Merry Christmas, sleepyheads!' she said. 'Breakfast before presents, remember!'

They scoffed their breakfast quickly and then stampeded through to the living room. OK, so the tree wasn't perfect – leaning a little, and decorated with badly painted pine cones – but Imogen still loved it. Beneath it was a stack of brightly packaged presents.

It didn't take long at all to unwrap them. Findlay got a new game for his console and a book about alligators, his new favourite animal (which Mum found strange). Imogen's best gift was a telescope from her gran. She wanted to go upstairs straight away and set it up, ready for that night so that she could see the stars even better. But as she was clearing up the wrapping paper, the doorbell rang.

'Who's that?' said Findlay.

Their mum had a strange smile on her face. 'I think it's Santa, come to deliver one more gift.'

'Ha, ha,' said Imogen.

'Why don't you go and see?'

Imogen stood up and went to the front door. When she opened it, Ciara was standing on the other side. 'Merry Christmas, Immy!' she said.

'Oh, hi!' said Imogen, confused.

It was a week since the incident at Pet Haven, and Imogen still felt guilty about hiding the truth. Everyone else – Ciara included – thought there had been a break-in. They were just grateful nothing had been taken and that all the animals were safe. Only Pirate had been out of his pen and everyone thought that somehow he had got out and seen the intruder off.

'Told you he was the cleverest and bravest dog here,' Ciara had said.

So, why was she on their doorstep now?

'Is everything OK?' asked Imogen.

'It's all fine,' said Ciara. 'I just came to give you this.'

She reached into her pocket and took out a metal disc, which she passed to Imogen. One side had their phone number written on it. She flipped it in her palm. The other side had one single word.

A warm tide spread from the soles of her feet, through her body, to the roots of her hair. She couldn't talk. She could hardly even *breathe*. She looked at Ciara's beaming smile and then turned to see her mum behind her, tears in her eyes.

'Mum?' she said, finally managing to speak. 'Really?'

'I know it's been hard this year,' Mum said. 'The

house feels empty without Dad. I know we can't replace him, but I thought we could all do with cheering things up a little.'

'Wait here,' said Ciara.

She walked back up the snow-covered drive and opened the boot of her estate car.

A black-and-white shape leapt out and Imogen called his name. Pirate spun on the spot, then saw her and began to bark. He darted across the lawn, paws kicking up snow, and skidded to a stop at her feet. His tail was wagging so hard that his bottom rocked back and forth. Imogen fell to her knees and wrapped her arms around him. She couldn't believe he was here, on *her* doorstep. She took his face in her hands.

'You're going to come and live with us,' she said. 'You're going to be my Pirate and I'll be your Imogen!'

He let out a yowl of excitement, then ran past, into the house, carrying clumps of snow with him.

Imogen felt like bursting into tears, but managed to hold it together. 'Thank you!' she said to Ciara. Then, 'Thank you,' to her mum. 'Thank you, thank you, thank you.'

'There's no need,' said her mum. 'Ciara's told me everything you do at the sanctuary. You've proven you're ready to have a pet.'

'He's not a *pet*, Mum,' she said sternly. 'He's a *companion*. He's chosen us! Remember, it's not ownership, it's companionship. He's part of our family now.'

'Sorry!' said her mum. She looked at the snowy paw prints on the floor. 'And he's certainly chosen to make a mess of my carpet . . . Another scruffy family member to look after!'

Ciara laughed and handed over a lead. 'I'll leave you to settle in,' she said. 'Merry Christmas, all!'

Imogen gave Ciara a massive hug, then said goodbye and thanked her again.

'Right, he needs a walk!' she said. She knew there was only one place she wanted to go with Pirate.

'Just in the back garden for now!' said Mum. 'Gran and Grandad will be here in a minute.'

'But, Mum . . .'

'You can take him out for a proper run after lunch,' said her mum.

Imogen just smiled. She didn't mind where she was or what she was doing now that Pirate was by her side.

* * *

Later that day, after lunch and more present-giving, they went on their walk, and there was still only one destination on Imogen's mind. As she and her brother approached the trees, she let Pirate off his lead. He darted ahead, then lay flat on his belly, waiting for them at the forest's edge.

'Good boy!' said Imogen. 'Makes a change from the same field every day, doesn't it?'

Pirate rolled over gleefully, then stood up and shook the flakes from his fur like a sprinkler.

Mum had said they had to be back in an hour, but Imogen had begged for two. Mum agreed, as long as they were home before it got dark.

The snow creaked under their wellies as they entered the forest. Imogen knew the way now like the back of her hand, and Findlay made snowballs, throwing them for Pirate to catch in his mouth.

'You know, I've been thinking,' he said. 'I might

318

move back into my room if that's OK with you?'

'I'll be fine,' she said, smiling to herself. 'We'll both be fine.'

Then she paused and a thought struck her.

'Remember what Daddy used to say – "Every little fear faced fills your heart with courage".'

Findlay nodded.

'Well, look at us now. And all thanks to Vetman.'

She called to Pirate and he dashed back to her side. 'I can't wait for you to meet Vetman. You'll love him, and he'll love you!' She stopped, as another thought occurred. 'There are some other animals there you might not have seen before.' Pirate cocked his head. 'But you mustn't be scared. I'll be right by your side. In fact, I think you'll get on with the kangaroo very well indeed!'

Pirate wagged his tail, and they continued. Imogen hadn't been able to come this way all week, since the night they'd left Vetman in his cocoon, but she'd thought about him and the bionic clan all the time.

She'd thought about Trevor as well. She had no idea where he'd gone or what he was going to do next, but his motorbike had disappeared from the sanctuary too. She wondered if he could really change. Despite his anger and all the heartache it had almost caused, she'd seen it wasn't only rage in his eyes as he fled the bunker. It was shame as well. And if he still wasn't ready to accept Vetman's extraordinary gift, that shame would sour inside him once more.

Vetman had shown her that shame stops us from seeing who we can really become. Christmas wasn't about receiving, but about giving with an open heart – unconditionally. Trevor's clothes might have been threadbare and tatty, but she realised that he wore his own armour too, reflecting the pain and trauma the world had inflicted on him. Like the bullies at school, he couldn't look in the mirror. She hoped he would accept Vetman's gift and let love in to take

the pain away. Even after all he'd done. As her dad
had said, he would need to be vulnerable so that he
might be strong again. She had been on that same
journey herself.

Her thoughts were interrupted as they reached the
clearing in the centre of the woods.

'Huh?' said Findlay.

Her brother was standing at the edge of the clearing,
where there should have been a cottage. Imogen's
feet carried her forward, but she didn't understand.
The ground was blanketed in pristine white snow.
There was no cottage, or any sign one had ever
stood there.

Findlay shook his head. 'This must be the wrong
place.'

Imogen knew it wasn't. The cottage, impossible
though it seemed, had simply vanished.

No, not impossible. No more than a flying suit of
armour, a hedgehog with bionic springs, a bat with

X-ray vision, a bear with excavator arms or a flying tortoise with a wheelbarrow for a shell that had rockets in the handles.

'He's gone,' she said.

'He can't be!' said Findlay, sounding angry. 'He said he'd be here. He said we could always find him.'

Pirate sniffed at the snow and gave an uncertain whine.

Imogen bent down to stroke his ears, but her heart felt hollow. Quite suddenly all the hope was scooped out of her. He *had* said that, hadn't he?

'He must have moved on,' she said.

'He can't just leave us!' said Findlay. 'Not like this.' He was close to tears, and Imogen didn't know what to say. It didn't seem fair to her either.

They both stood there for a few seconds, lost and bewildered.

'We should go home,' Imogen said sadly. 'Come on. It'll be dark soon.'

She pulled on Pirate's leash, but he was sniffing the ground. She tugged again; he wouldn't budge. 'What is it, boy?' she said. 'We really need to go.'

Pirate stood right where he was, pawing the ground and wagging his tail. Imogen looked down and at first it seemed like a trick of the twilight. But then there was no mistaking – there in the undergrowth was a tiny vial of dust radiating every colour of the rainbow, and then some other colours as well, which Imogen didn't even know the names of. She picked it up and turned it in her hand. She recognised its contents from the operation on their hedgehog friend, the first time they'd entered the bunker and Vetman's world of wonders.

'Bionic dust,' she said. 'The stardust of unconditional love.'

As she held it out for Findlay to see, a light spatter of snow tickled her face. More landed across Pirate's back. She looked up and saw a branch trembling, sending a cascade of icy flakes down upon them. She blinked them away. On the branch, watching them as the blanket of dusk descended from above, was the squirrel with the metal brush tail. Pirate barked, but the squirrel didn't stir. She took a good long look at them and almost seemed to be smiling.

'It's OK, Pirate,' said Findlay with a grin. 'She's Vetman's friend too.'

The squirrel twitched, before bouncing from branch to branch, spilling snow as she went.

'Come back!' Imogen called, taking a step in pursuit. The squirrel either didn't listen or didn't hear, and Imogen's gaze lost the bristly tail as it vanished in the canopy above. She stared into the treetops, willing her to reappear. But as disappointment settled in her stomach, her eyes found something else, snagging on a single bright point between the branches, the first of the stars to prick the deepening blue of the dusk sky. The brightest star.

'That's our star,' she said to Pirate, pointing upwards. 'The Dog Star!'

His tail wagged, and she thought he understood, at least a little.

She clutched the vial of stardust and thought of her dad, looking down. Always with them.

'You know, Finn,' she said. 'Daddy always told me love is in the stars.' Her brother stared at her, listening. 'I used to think it was just an old saying – a way to make me feel less sad . . . but now I know better.'

Findlay nodded with a kind of wisdom in his eyes that Imogen hadn't seen before. In the fading light, he looked older than his years.

'Just like Vetman,' he said, gesturing at the vial in her hand. 'His stardust is like love. It heals everything.'

Imogen smiled at him and nodded, then took his gloved hand. 'Let's go home before Mum starts to worry.'

She remembered Vetman's words in her head – what she had been searching for was inside her all along. She found a hero who helped her conquer her fear and now she felt she could be a hero for herself, for Findlay, for Mum and for all the animals. She didn't need a suit of armour – she could be whoever she wanted to be. She was sure of it now.

As they walked back through the trees, the Dog Star seemed to guide them. They were no longer alone or afraid of anything. Slowly, the other stars joined, and by the time they reached home the sky was ablaze with dappled silver starlight. Mum didn't seem to mind that they were a little bit late. With the arrival of Pirate, for some reason that didn't need to be spoken about, Imogen had gone from a twelve-year-old child to a nearly thirteen-year-old responsible dog guardian in the space of one afternoon.

As they took off their wellingtons and coats at the front door, Pirate waited patiently on the step.

'He's learning already!' said Mum, handing Imogen a towel.

Imogen dried off Pirate's damp paws and fur, stroking his ears and telling him how clever he was. All the time, he stared straight into her eyes with a look of deep, unconditional love. He knew her own eyes told him exactly the same.

Then, like a bolt of lightning, it hit her. How had she not noticed before? Pirate's eyes were emerald green too – bottomless pools of kindness.

Her heart surged as she finally understood.

Vetman's cottage had vanished. He might have disappeared to some other place, or even some other planet. But love was everywhere, if you knew where to look – especially in the eyes of an animal friend. It was the love of an animal that had helped her find Vetman in the first place – and to find out what she herself could become along the way. He believed in her, and now she believed in herself. As long as she had unconditional love in her heart, Vetman would always be with her.

He was by her side. Now, before, and for every day onwards.

Author's Note

During the final days of preparation of this
manuscript, I lost my beloved companion of
nearly 14 years, an incredible and amazing
little Border Terrier, Keira.
She was never mine – I was hers.
We shared mutual respect and companionship.

I read this story to her out loud, as she lay at
my feet and I made the last changes. I didn't
know those were to be her last days.
I feel very blessed and lucky to have had her in my
life, lighting the way with her magnificent
unconditional love.
She inspired everything I do for animals and her
legacy will be eternal.
My heart is truly broken. She was my best friend in
the whole wide world.

As Imogen said, 'Pain is love,
and love is pain – that's just how it is.'
With great love comes great pain.
But in spite of the heartache, her love is the most
wonderful gift I have ever experienced.
She saved me from myself and inspired me to be
the best I could become.

Thank you, my beautiful baby girl.
May you run in the stars forever.
I give you back to the oneness.
Your light remains inside me.

You are by my side.
Now, before, and for every day onwards.

I love you beyond words.
Noel xxx

Professor Noel Fitzpatrick

is a world-renowned veterinary surgeon, the founder of
Fitzpatrick Referrals in Surrey, and the star of
the hit Channel 4 television show *The Supervet*,
now in its seventeenth series.

When Noel was a child, he dreamt up Vetman
as a hero who would save all the broken and
discarded animals of the world and make them well
again using amazing inventions made from the things
other people throw away. He's incredibly excited
to share the story of his hero with readers.

Noel lives in Surrey with his Maine Coon cats
Ricochet and Excalibur, and you can follow him at:
Facebook: @ProfessorNoelFitzpatrick
Twitter: @ProfNoelFitz
Instagram: @ProfNoelFitzpatrick